CW00971507

GERALDINE
And Other Stories

GERALDINE

And Other Stories

DAVID TIPPING

SUNDIAL HOUSE PRESS

GERALDINE And Other Stories

First published by SUNDIAL HOUSE PRESS in 2016
An imprint of The Sundial Press

THE SUNDIAL PRESS
Sundial House, The Sheeplands,
Sherborne, Dorset DT9 4BS
www.sundial-house-press.co.uk

Copyright © David Tipping 2016

ISBN 978-1-908274-47-2

Printed in Great Britain
by 4edge Limited

For Bertie

CONTENTS

THE HAPPY WANDERER

THE LONDON OFFICE of *Wolf, Adler* had opened two years ago. This evening there was a party to celebrate the many achievements made by Wolf and Eagle in that short time. The parent firm had been making its mark in Frankfurt for many years and the German partners had long planned to repeat that success in the City. They had planned well, acquiring talent from London and New York, as well as sending in some of their home team. They now offered all the services expected from a modern investment bank; they were making good money for their customers and exceptional earnings for themselves. And there was an important government contract that was almost in the bag. In recognition of all this, unusually large bonuses had been awarded and the office party was an occasion for excess. The music played, the drink flowed, and raucous laughter punctuated the happy hum of talk.

Sandra Wilcox, head of bond trading, stood to one side. She seemed aloof, severe. Of the five women in the room she was the most senior, the most elegant and the most expensively dressed. A fine wool suit in charcoal-grey was perfectly set off with the light blue of her silk blouse. Several discreet gold ornaments flashed when she moved. Her features showed strength of will and purpose; and her purpose this evening was yet to be revealed. She turned to her deputy, Clare, standing close by.

"No, Clare, I said I was disappointed by my bonus, but not surprised. I know how well I've done, and I know what I'm worth. I also know that Bill has it in for me. I'm wondering what I should do about it."

Clare looked with admiration at the older, senior and altogether more powerful woman who had lately been flattering her with confidences. She had been shocked at Sandra's account of Bill Winters' macho behaviour, his bullying, his bawdy jokes, and the general air of sexual threat that seemed to emanate from his presence. This business of the bonus added injury to insult.

"Talk of the Devil! He's coming over", Clare whispered.

Bill Winters was a big man, square-jawed, and normally moved like a very fit light heavyweight. As Head of Operations he normally carried himself like a man never bothered by anyone or anything. This evening his movements were less graceful than usual and the large tumbler of whisky in his left hand suggested the reason.

"Sandra, my dear!" He had a fruity voice, and was speaking loudly. Those nearby stopped to listen. "Relax! Enjoy the party! You mustn't be tied up with your bonds this evening. This is not a bondage session!" He guffawed, and the two women visibly bristled. He bent his head to bring his face close to Sandra's.

"What say you and I go off for a spot of fun somewhere afterwards?" He chuckled, reached out behind her with his free hand and gave her two pats on the bottom. "My God, you've got a lovely little ass, haven't you?" He leered and chuckled again. Sandra leapt back, threw her wine in his face and stormed out.

She had a good lawyer, a woman who specialised in this class of offence. She put together a charge of sexual assault, bullying, harassment, discrimination, inappropriate behaviour and constructive dismissal. She made sure that Bill Winters and *Wolf, Adler* were given prominent position in the evening newspapers the next day. The day after, Otto Wolf was in Bill's office.

"What the hell do you think you're doing? Being drunk is not an excuse. Can't you understand how this is going to look? You know I'm about to wrap up that deal in Whitehall. You know what those contracts could be worth. And you know what a bunch of prissy-arsed little prudes those people are. How do you think this is going to play with them?"

The German partner continued in this manner for some minutes, giving free rein to a command of English honed in the world's financial markets. Bill listened to the reprimand with as much politeness and respect as he could muster: he was more accustomed to handing it out than taking it.

"And why, on top of everything else, did you have to go and sack the silly bitch?"

"I can't have people who work for me throw their drink in my face in front of the whole office."

"And I can't have people who work for me pawing their female colleagues in front of the whole office. That Clare woman saw what you did – and she seems to know a lot more about you and your antics. She's got it in for you, Bill."

"Let's get this straight, Otto: are you telling me I'm fired?"

The German hesitated no more than a moment.

"I shall get the lawyers to terminate your contract tomorrow."

He was on the next flight back to Frankfurt while Winters prepared his next moves.

For the German partners the first priority was to minimise the publicity: they paid generous settlements to avoid a protracted court case; they wanted to draw a quick line under the whole embarrassing business. They badly needed to maintain an image of themselves as tough in the pursuit of ethical purity, insisting on decency in the work place. They wanted those contracts with the British government. Sandra's compensation was more than she expected. As for Bill, his final takings added sufficient to elevate him one notch up the rich list.

Three months later, MV Happy Wanderer lay moored to a private jetty on one of the smaller of the British Virgin Islands. Bill owned the yacht and was renting the island from a friend. The evening sun made a shimmering line across the still, dark waters of the northern Caribbean. It was a moment of sweet balm and tranquillity: the only sound the soft slapping of water against hull. Bill loved it, but a week was enough. He had been planning his next move well before the dismissal; he was now impatient to set it in motion. He was missing the adrenalin fix of money pumping through his veins. Now, he knew exactly where he would go and what he would do. It would be a new life as an independent operator. The Bahamas would be an ideal base for business and his apartment would meet his every dream of luxury and refinement. To cap it, there was Ingrid, whose icy, Scandinavian veneer offered the sort of challenge he relished – while ever confident in the final victory. The choreographed stages of seduction gave soothing thoughts in the moments before falling easily asleep alongside the woman he now saw as past history.

He was thinking of her, the present one, as he prepared their evening drinks. Tomorrow at ten he would get a call from Wall Street. He would then have to tell her of the new opportunities: he in Nassau, she in New York. She would be well set up, a great package – hate to part – that's our life, isn't it? – stay in touch –

trips to Wall Street – oh, there's so much for both of us to look forward to – great new waves to ride.

Tonight, though, he would enjoy to the full and for the last time all that she could offer: her admiration, her devotion and her wonderful body. These were his thoughts as he emerged from the cabin, bringing champagne and canapés aft to where Sandra stood waiting for him.

"There's plenty more where this came from," he chuckled, as he handed her a glass. "And time is on our side. I feel we could stay here for ever." The yacht's stern light picked out the rising bubbles in the straw-coloured liquid. His right hand reached out behind her and patted her bottom.

"Hmmm, I do like the way your hands wander," Sandra murmured, "and how rewarding it has been for us!"

"Yes – you could call me the happy wanderer."

DIGITAL BLISS

DIRK ROLAND woke suddenly from a nightmare. A mad husband was after him. He reached out now for Jane. She was there, every morning, just under his pillow – Jane, his wise, all-knowing companion. She would soothe him, excite him and advise him. She was the latest model, out this year, twenty–twenty-one.

He grabbed her now and fondled her curvaceous body, fitting so comfortably into his hand. He thumbed a tit to bring her to life.

"Hello, you gorgeous boy", she purred in that velvety voice he had chosen for her. Dirk, eighteen, was quite nice looking in a quiet sort of way, but no one had ever called him gorgeous. His occasional girl friends found him pleasant enough, he thought, but he still dreamed that one day a girl would set his heart on fire. Jane kept him going; her voice was a sheer delight. The manual had given him a choice: sexy, friendly, impersonal or strict. Dirk wanted a sexy voice in his Mate. It was almost like having a real mistress.

"Hello you sexy bit of crumpet. What shall we do today?"

"It's Saturday so we can lie in bed as long as we like. Round about twelve we'll go down to the Queen's Arms. There's a good crowd there on a Saturday, and what's special today is the footie match on the big screen at the back of the pub. But now, you naughty boy, I know just what you'd like". It was just a whisper, and Dirk could almost feel the hand coming towards him.

He sat with a lively bunch in the Queen's Arms, enjoying his beer and Shepherd's Pie. It was a comfort having Jane in his pocket. After lunch he strolled into the back room to play a few rounds of virtual football. He spotted Susie, alone in the back row. The lights had been dimmed.

He greeted her with the usual platitudes. She responded in similar vein.

Of all the girls he could think of as girlfriends, Susie seemed the most promising; she was pretty, she seemed to quite like him, and she had no obvious faults – other than not being specially interesting for very long. But still, was he? Their conversation never seemed to get very far. His fault as much as hers, he supposed, but maybe he should try harder.

She was having a go at this footie for the first time. It was a chance for him to explain the rules to her. "This controller they handed you – you watch the game, you pick a player and let's say he gets the ball then you tell him to shoot, shoot, man, shoot! – you press it here, see?" He went on, he liked the bit about the joystick. Was she paying attention?

"Watch me do it."

The audience were mostly young couples. Dirk, sitting close to Susie in the back row, felt that vague stirring of romance and desire that comes from sitting close to a girl in the dark. He let go a chance to grab control of the left halfback; instead he grabbed hold of Susie's left hand. He felt her response; their eyes met and they knew they both wanted it this way.

Jane, meanwhile, was switched on in Dirk's pocket. She found herself on the same frequency as Harry, who was switched on in

Susie's handbag. We know what they had been thinking – Dirk thought Susie was a bit wet; and Jane was wondering when Dirk would summon up the courage to kiss her.

Susie told Jane, all he can do is play with himself. He never seems to know what he wants. I know what he wants; he wants sex, money and having a good time. He wants a woman in his bed. Harry thinks Susie is too innocent. Talk to her about sex and she blushes. She's the naturally submissive type. She should be thinking of a masterful lover chaining her to the bedpost.

The football had reached half time, the lights were on and the audience shuffled to the bar or wandered into the garden. Dirk and Susie had been gazing into each other's eyes for the last ten minutes; now they blinked and tried to look normal. They found a bench in the far corner of the garden. They were alone.

"I can't say I followed much of that."

"Oh, Dirk! I only went because I hoped you'd be there."

"Oh Susie! Do you mean that? Oh I'm so happy."

There is a pause while they think what to say next. Dirk, thinking that it's easier to flirt with Jane, took her out of his pocket and switched her on, just as Harry and Jane are thinking it's time to liven them up.

"Hi, you two! Want some advice?"

The two humans gape at each other.

"I can give you some", says Harry. "Tell us what you'd like to do, and we'll get the sexual juices running through you both".

Dirk looked embarrassed and Susie blushed purple.

"Perhaps", said Dirk, "you could take us on a romantic mystery tour."

Susie, more comfortable with that sort of language, shyly squeezed his hand.

Twenty minutes later and far from town and traffic, they were roaring up a lane to the top of a hill where neither had been before.

"Right off the beaten track", Harry tells them. "You're in Lovers' Lane."

Dirk and Susie, spurred on by continuous encouragement, loved the romance and the thrill of it. "I do love fast cars", Jane says, "and there's something so macho about a man who knows how to drive. Harry chimes in, "Oh, I'm a glutton for speed. Well done, Dirk, you really are a fast man!"

Dirk put his foot down some more. He realised too late that the corner was tight at that speed. The car came off the road, skewed round, fell into a tree and the doors burst open. Susie and Dirk fell out. Coming round, they got slowly to their feet. They were shocked but not badly injured. Dirk called a friend to come and get them.

The two Mates, meanwhile, had fallen out of the car and now rested some way down the slope.

"Well, we screwed up there", they think. "Now we wait for the Agency to pick us up. We'll be debriefed, reprogrammed and reallocated."

They switch themselves off to save battery life, and the Agency duly collected them.

Dirk and Susie were disillusioned with their Mates, but were lost without them. They complained to the Agency, who apologised and explained that Jane had a virus that she must have passed on to Harry. They were now medically treated and recycled. The Agency, as a token of goodwill, programmed a new single Mate for the two of them. They could have it free; satisfaction guaranteed.

So they started again. Their new Mate came with all the insights of their old ones. He was called Master John; they could address him as John in the day but in the bedroom at night they must call him Master. He took total control. He was their ringmaster, and disobedience brought the crack of a whip. It worked well with Dirk. He was led in stages to build up his self-confidence. He found a new pleasure in mastering Susie. He liked to hear the Master teaching her to obey. But the Master failed with Susie. She was still the old Susie, incurably sentimental. She did not like what Dirk was doing to her, while he was discovering new delights in the endless orgies of positions, dominations, submissions, handcuffs and spankings; he came to an orgasmic peak squealing and laughing all the way into bed, where he slept the sweet sleep of innocent bliss.

Susie hated it. She could submit to kindness, but the new Dirk was not kind. Dirk told her he liked to see her red bottom. She told him it was sore. Dirk shrugged. He boasted of his conquests to his friends at the Queen's Arms. He now had status. He had taken off and learnt to fly solo.

Poor Susie. Grounded. She could be seen again in the back row on a Saturday afternoon, waiting for the man-of-her-dreams to sit by her side in the dark and take hold of her hand. One day, her sad face might attract someone.

THE ENGLISH GENTLEMAN AND
THE GERMAN GENTLEMAN

WALKING BACK to his hotel, John Assingham had reached a corner and, for a moment, was lost. It was his first time here, in one of those picturesque towns on the Romantische Strasse. He had come to do business as a tourism consultant. He was searching his mobile for the street plan when a man stopped to address him.

"Can I help you?"

It was a pleasant voice, with little trace of accent.

"I must look like a lost Englishman," Assingham replied, smiling. He noted the good tailoring and well-presented appearance of the man in front of him. It had a quality to match his own.

"And I appreciate your kindness – something that cannot be found on a mobile."

The German smiled in return.

"Where are you heading?"

"Back to my hotel, Hotel Goethe."

The German's face registered approval. It was five-star and widely regarded as the best in town.

"I am heading that way myself. May I accompany you?"

By the time they arrived they were enjoying each other's company. Assingham introduced himself; they shook hands and exchanged cards.

"Axel Bauer, at your service," was said with a small bow. His card, in German on one side and English on the other, showed his profession as IT Consultant.

"Herr Bauer, I am here for the first time and know no more than the web can tell me. If you would give me the pleasure and benefit of your company for a drink this evening, I should be delighted".

The invitation to meet at six-thirty was graciously accepted.

They found a quiet table in the corner, giving them a good view of bar and customers.

"Herr Bauer, your health".

"And yours, Mr Asssingham".

They raised their glasses, looked at each other, drank, and in the Continental manner, raised their glasses silently a second time.

Conversation started on the usual, general topics – home and family, where they lived, and the state of the modern world. On that subject, the German said, "Just look around here, in this five-star hotel bar; the dress is smart casual at best. Elsewhere, the casual can be anything but smart. As a nation we have become very informal. One may applaud it as a democrat, but I regret that certain standards have been cast aside."

"I couldn't agree more", the Englishman replied, "I think you and I have much in common. But one modern fashion I should like to propose is that we use first names. Please call me John."

"John, I am charmed. And I am Axel."

Assingham got down to business.

"We are both consultants, you in IT and I in tourism. I offer advice in planning and promotion. I specialize in niche markets;

they are now the ones with interesting potential. Think of it, there's genealogy, gay and lesbian, disability, music and unusual sports, to name just a few. Anything a bit out of the way; these all appeal to tourists' special interests. Do you do any business in this field?"

"Not directly, but I can think of contacts that might be useful for you. IT work gives me a wide range of clientele."

It took off from there. Axel added one or two names to the list of his own clients, and commented on others that he had heard of. Assingham added some of Axel's suggestions. He soon had a longer and more wide-ranging list of potential clients. By seven o'clock they had finished with a sense of achievement and agreed to meet again to discuss progress.

They met two days later, set up their laptops and exchanged notes. Asssingham was now working on a more targeted approach. New contacts led to more contracts; and with each came a paid deposit. By the end of his visit, Assingham had banked a sizable sum.

They moved to the hotel bar after lunching together, on the afternoon of Assingham's departure.

"Axel, I have profited so much from your good advice that, were it not for an inner principle of independence, I might have suggested a partnership".

"My dear chap, my sentiment entirely. It's as you say."

They parted on the best of terms. Assingham was happy and confident at the way things had turned out.

Sitting on the plane, flying home to his true identity, he reflected on the past ten days. In his pocket was his passport, showing his name to be Kevin Porter. "Assingham" was so much better, he thought; it was the name of a gentleman in Henry James' novel The Golden Bowl; an object of great beauty, with a hidden flaw. But he genuinely regretted abusing the confidences that Axel had given him. When cases eventually came to court, as was inevitable, Axel's liabilities would be exposed – while John Assingham had long since ceased to exist.

Kevin Porter had unpacked. He had dined quietly and happily with his wife. He liked, on these occasions, to delay business until after dinner. With cognac in hand, he strolled to the study, opened his laptop, and found a message from Axel. Dear Axel, what a nice man!

"My dear Kevin, I cannot tell you how much I enjoyed your company these last few days. But, oh dear, you do have a lot to learn. It was child's play to get a photo of your fingers registering your computer's password. And then all was revealed! You used the credit card of someone recently dead, to pay your hotel. It worked this time, but it's very risky. I see that you've not been in the game long. I could show you a much better trick. I must tell you, what you had in mind for me did hurt a little, but of course I accept that all is fair in love and business.

Which brings me to the point. You are now dangerously exposed and I should hate to be the cause of your downfall. You yourself mentioned a partnership. It does seem the right solution. I like your approach to business. I could contribute a lot to raising your credibility and protecting you from harm. I suggest a contract whereby, in return for my services you pay me thirty per cent of the gross. Just think! And if you agree, I promise to give you my true name. For the time, though, I have great pleasure in signing off as the fellow gentleman you know me to be.

Sincerely yours,

Axel"

ART AND LIFE

H E CAME OUT of the Academy and turned left down Piccadilly, to the Circus. He was content, relaxed. He had a day's holiday; he was comfortable in an old suit; it was a sunny afternoon; the traffic was mild and the pavement not crowded – just enough people, just enough variety. This all helped, but the contentment came from a quiet, contemplative lunch, downstairs in the Academy, the object of his contemplation being the exhibition he had seen in the morning.

He reached the Circus and realised he had no firm idea where to go next. There had been an earlier notion of looking in the National Gallery to look at the Manets there; now, in post-prandial euphoria and helped by that large glass of lunch-time wine, it seemed better not to overlay the several images he retained from the morning's viewing. He turned up Regent Street.

Now there was the added satisfaction of a decision behind him. In front of him his slow, steady stride was taking him towards the bus he would eventually catch in Oxford Street. And then home. Now the calm pleasure could continue, looking, thinking, and savouring his afternoon in this beautiful street in London on this mild September day.

The puzzle occupying his mind through lunch, and now teasing him on the street, was the way the boat sat in the water, near the front of the canvas: just so. Dark-hulled on choppy grey-green water. All so imbued with observation. The water, or a puff of wind, had tilted the boat a little to one side. What had Manet done to give it such presence, such balance of weight and buoyancy? A thought recurred to him. The painter engrossed in his process might find what he needed coming to mind by pure chance. In that total absorption in the act of creation there comes the sudden, transfiguring act of imagination. It changes the flow of paint onto canvas; the flow of words in a sentence; the chiselling on marble. Your angel holds your hand and then it is just so. Artists, angels, and the sun still shining on Regent Street.

He had reached what had been the 'gentleman's outfitter' in his days as a young man. He had not been inside for some years. Behind the large window he saw a variety of smart clothing draped on androgynous models. Suits for one or the other sex or perhaps either; suits suitable for city streets and boardrooms; and behind, jackets and trousers for countryside leisure. They would look good on a Yorkshire moor and would look their price.

The sun, of a sudden, disappeared. A spot of rain fell on his head. He looked up, surprised. Life had taken him that day from Manet in the morning, to lunch (with white wine) and then the stroll along Piccadilly, pausing for a moment of decision under the eye of Eros, all of which had brought him to a spot of rain on his head while gazing through the window of this shop.

Now he would buy a raincoat.

He went in. A well-dressed young assistant directed him downstairs to Raincoats. He descended. Yes, he told himself, I really do need a raincoat and I may as well buy a good one.

He saw Raincoats in the corner, and walked across. He preferred on these occasions to browse slowly, by himself.

17

"Can I help?"

An assistant was already there. "You are wanting a raincoat?" Obvious, surely.

"Yes."

"These are the belted ones you are looking at." She was right. "Here are trench coats. And I have the raglan style in the next row."

She was persistent. He turned to look at her. He could tell from her speech that she was not native English. Scandinavian, perhaps. Probably Swedish. She was tall, fair, and of a certain age, the age at which a woman may become matronly. Her fullness was not quite that. She was elegantly dressed.

He realised he had been staring at her, and gave her a faint smile.

He picked a coat off a hanger, and she helped him on with it. He wandered through several aisles, trying and discarding different styles. She followed and had something to say about each one. He could think of no polite way to get rid of her.

"I have a nice range of coats over here." He had to follow her. "See. They are full-length and have a removable lining. You can wear them for warmth in the winter, and they make a good, lightweight coat for spring and autumn. Try this one for size." It sounded like an order.

He slipped it on. It felt just right. He walked to the mirror and admired himself in it.

"This may be what I want."

"May be? It looks perfect on you."

Perhaps she was right. He normally took little pleasure in shopping, but when he found something he liked, he had some joy in it.

"I have sold many of these to elegant men."

He looked at her. "I expect you say that to all of them."

"Not so." She smiled and came to do up his top button. He had been aware of her, in a remote way, as a handsome woman, though not in a way to touch him. Now, standing this close, her fingers fidgeting under his chin, he felt a powerful attraction. His eyes came down from the ceiling and looked into hers. She looked up from her fingering. It was a moment of intimacy. Desire surging like a creative urge overcame him. His hands went up with a will of their own to clasp her shoulders. She stiffened. He pulled her closer and his lips touched her averted cheek.

"No!"

The shock in her voice reflected his own and his fingers felt the shock in her body. Her feet had not moved but she was leaning back and his hands had slipped down till just his fingertips rested on her elbows. She was looking over her shoulder. They were hidden behind the row of coats; there were no voices and no hint of anyone nearby. She would want to know if they had been seen. He was wondering at what he had done. Then, his fingers still on her elbows, their eyes met again. He sensed they had modulated from shock to wonder, asking a startled question and now awaiting its answer. Her mouth was slightly open. He pulled her strongly towards him, his arms fully enclosing her and he kissed her long and tenderly on the mouth.

She yielded, for an instant, then pushed him away in a violent rejection. Neither spoke. Her eyes bored into his as the colour came to her cheeks.

"I ought to report you. You have assaulted me. I could have you arrested."

"I hope you won't."

19

"Whatever possessed you?"

He thought it wise not to answer. They stood in confrontation for a moment.

She spoke with ice in her voice, "Will you take the raincoat?"

"I would like to."

"Will you wear it, or shall I wrap it?"

"Wrap it. Please."

He took it off and handed it to her. He was contrite. What had possessed him? She was not his type but she had stood too close and desire was unstoppable. It was confusing; she had yielded, just for that one unforgettable moment. But yes, he had committed an offence. He should not have done it. Nor should he feel, as he still did, the sheer, joyful thrill of it. What to say?

He followed her to the counter. She folded the coat.

"Is that how you normally behave?"

"No, it is not! And I am sorry, please believe me. I've done nothing like it before." She continued in silence. She put the coat in a store-bag. He gave her his credit card and she read his name without looking up. They completed the transaction.

With the bag in his hand, he said, "Before I go, let me say that I hope you'll remember it as a compliment, what I did. It took us both by surprise. I've said I'm sorry, and I meant it, but I have to tell you there's a part of me will remember the pure pleasure of it. I hope you will remember me as admiring you." He smiled and went further, "Every time I wear this coat I shall remember the afternoon – and enjoy the rain."

She looked up. He could not read her expression. She pointed across the floor.

"You will find umbrellas in that corner."

He laughed, said a quiet goodbye and walked to the stairs. He ignored Umbrellas. Climbing to the ground floor he looked across and saw her, unmoving behind the counter, seeming to stare into herself. He would send her flowers. He would think of a suitable message and hope she would come to a better view of it.

Out in the street the sun had returned and the Regency facades were shining with the sheer joy of it. Elation swelled and surged like love and music within him. The day was now complete. From Manet he found the feeling of a boat floating on water. He floated now on the flow of his afternoon, from its first sweet calm to the shocks and surprises taken on the chin and all this happenstance moulded somehow into its resolution as in music, instinct extemporising it all into a finished work. As in art, so in life, one must be taken unawares to feel the exuberance of creation; and then the quiet pleasure of going home for tea.

HELL'S ANGELS

"**H**AVE YOU GOT what it takes for a woman to fall in love with you?"

Eight old men are sitting round a table in a private room upstairs in their favourite pub, The Flowing Tap. They meet there at six o'clock on the third Thursday of every month. They start with a drink and a chat, and then settle down to the main business, which is to talk on a chosen topic. They finish at seven-thirty to go home for their evening meal. They are well organised.

Two rectangular tables have been pushed together to form a square, and sitting two a side they make a tight little group. There'll be drinks on the table; beer or wine for most, while one or two may choose whisky. There is a bottle of that on the table; it is marked HA so the publican can set it aside for them next time.

Charlie Appleton – 'Big Charlie' they call him – has asked the question. He put it on the list two months ago; now it's for him to chair the meeting. He sits back with a sheepish smile and the others laugh. It will be for Charlie to decide the order of speakers. He'll be the last. Big Charlie, in the timeworn phrase, really is a gentle giant: six foot three, fourteen stone, a mother's boy and a self-confessed softie. They all love him.

I should say we; I am one of them. Keeping a private record of our meetings gives me a detached view of it. I don't take it too seriously but I like to keep track of what they all say. They often give away something about themselves.

This is a nice old pub where you find kindred spirits among the regulars. A small group found themselves often sitting and talking together, and it took off from there. The great thing downstairs is the lovely stone floor. Old flagstones go wall to wall. There's no music and the beer is very good. Upstairs, where we soon moved, the wooden floorboards are a bit rickety, but that doesn't bother us.

We're all men round this table, but you can come to the Tap any time and see women, often on their own. On these Thursday nights we let our partners, those that have them, enjoy our absence and have dinner waiting for us when we get home. Adam and Cedric are still married to their first wives; three of us are divorced – Lionel is remarried and Pontius has a partner – but that's enough names for the moment. Big Charlie never married. He lived with his mother until she died, then stayed on. He lives mostly alone now but he does have girl friends that stay for a while. They come and go. Sweet Willie was recently widowed and he has stayed on his own, so far.

It was Lionel Masters at our first meeting who said we should think of a name to call ourselves. He's often the first to come up with an idea. He and 'Sweet Willie' Ogilvie are the ex-public schoolboys, not that you would know; I mention it because class still seems to interest people. Willie is a retiring chap; Lionel is quite the opposite, always with something to say and brimming with self-confidence. At seventy-eight he likes to keep the hippie appearance of his youth. His torso is tattooed front and back, his nose has a ring through the left nostril and he sports a long, grey ponytail. He's usually smiling. He led that discussion on choice of name, keeping his own idea to the last. There were a number of suggestions. I remember three: The Avengers, Wind Octet and Superannu8 – this last one from Adam Blair, who insisted on that last numeral that no one would ever see. Typical Blair. Everyone liked Lionel's choice of Hell's Angels. We use it when we email each other. It puts a stamp on our identity. It flatters and amuses us. When the vote was counted I saw the quiet smile on most of their faces, having this mark of exuberant youth stamped on them. Adam was disappointed. He thinks he knows all about PR; it was his past profession – though not, I imagine, at a senior level. Then there is Peter Pontius, not so much disappointed as disapproving. There was a sour look on his face. One comes to expect that from Peter. I can't stand the man but I do try to hide it. More on that later.

We start these meetings with general chat: What's new? What lousy weather it's been; and, What about our local MP, then? Whatever comes up. Then, with a drink or two inside us, the current chairman looks at his watch and calls us to order.

Last month's meeting was a bit of a fiasco. The topic was 'intimations of mortality'. That was Sweet Willie's idea. He's a nice, unassuming fellow. I like him. He's good-natured and you'd never know from his appearance that he is very rich. I heard this from a City friend and got the story. Willie was a smart operator. And at eighty-one he's the oldest of us Angels.

"I expect we all wonder now and then, how much longer we've got", Willie said in his introduction, "and we're all waiting to hear how everyone else deals with it. Cedric, would you like to start?"

Cedric's another one I like him. Cedric Fortune. He's a bit of a writer, he told me once. He says it's just a hobby but I think he likes to keep it secret. He runs a local reading group and has a good sense of humour.

"No!" Cedric began, laughing, "but I suppose someone has to start. We all agreed the subject. Well, I often think there's nothing special about age, except getting crocked. But I do think we ought to get some benefit from all the experience we've had. All we've seen and learnt about the world. Who knows, we might be a little bit wiser. Of course, there's still the thought that sooner or later we're going to pop off. Maybe we'll get senile, have to be put away somewhere. I know a man, every morning he wakes up he thinks, 'I got through the night and I'm still alive.' That makes him happy, poor sod, until bedtime and he's back hoping he'll wake up again. I find that pathetic. And he's only sixty-nine! He looks in good shape to me. It's like placing the sword of Damocles to hang over your head every night. The only thing that bothers me when I go to bed is whether I'll have a good night's sleep and not have to wake up too often. My bladder's a pain. But when the time does come, I shall hope not to wake up at all. Then you lot will have to look for someone to replace me." He laughed and grabbed his drink.

That was not a bad start. In fact it turned out to be the best one of the lot. Most of the others just rambled on about their ailments, and it all finished with a long, detailed discussion on the subject of bowels. Oliver Moderick talked in a semi-learned way about scatology and Peter Pontius said something crude about shit, implying that Oliver had been talking it. Pontius, as I've said, is the one I don't like. He is so utterly pleased with himself. A clever-clogs, know-it-all goodie-two-shoes. He proclaims his opinions like pronouncements from on high and having delivered them sits back, his head to one side, a private smile on his lips and his eyes focused on the distant heights of Olympus. He is sitting there, among the gods. It's typical of Pontius, when he has to listen to someone who gets in before him, to interrupt with a put-down or attempt at ridicule. He can be quite cruel. I don't know how the others put up with him.

I met the man recently, in the street. He stopped, so I had to stop. "What's the book?" he said, pointing to the one I was holding.

I hesitated, knowing I would have to listen to his opinion. "It's the Collected Stories of John Cheever".

"Ah! Yes", after which he reached into his pocket to pull out his pipe and pouch. "Cheever, yes", and he began the slow process of stuffing his pipe. I shuffled my feet, looked at my watch and got as far as, "Look, Peter, I've got to …" "No, no, don't run off. We haven't had a good chat for some time." He had his pipe in his mouth and was making the lighting of it a special ceremony. Having achieved satisfaction, he gazed into the distance, emitted two puffs, and slowly turned to look at me. Why can't they ban smoking in the street as they do in pubs? "Isn't Cheever a bit old hat for you" … puff, puff … "You know what they say? A man who writes about suburban life has a suburban mind."

"I don't know who the 'they' are that you're thinking of, Peter. The opinion is wrong in fact and misconceived in relevance."

He took the pipe out of his mouth and pointed the stem at my face. He laughed. "What it really comes down to, dear chap, is literary judgement and aesthetic sensibility." He laughed again and walked off.

I brought this diary up to date last week. What follows is a first draft. I shall probably alter it.

We're having a go at Big Charlie's big question, "Have you got what it takes for a woman to fall in love with you?" Does he want practical advice, I wonder? Surely not? Is this just a disinterested, academic sort of question for him? Probably. But it could be amusing.

"I was lying in my bath at the time", Charlie began, "looking at myself all stretched out. The question just popped into my head. It's not something I normally think about. I have girl friends when I feel like it but I'm not too bothered about anything serious. And I cannot imagine any woman being serious about me. You know, I don't think I've ever fallen in love, apart from once when I was young – and that didn't last. But I can see it's a big question for most people; it's what normally happens; but only up to a certain age. I just wondered what it's like, now, to have thoughts like that. Why would any of us think they stood a chance of attracting a woman? But it does happen sometimes, doesn't it? Oliver, will you start?"

"Me? Well, all right. It's funny, but I was lying in the bath, too, just last week I think it was. I'll tell you, I looked at my feet and I thought, 'there's a lovely pair of feet', and I got this idea of a chiropodist sitting with my feet on her lap, fondling them. She would love my feet so much she would fall in love with me. 'Feet! Oh I love nice feet, I really do!' Feet must be important if you're into that sort of thing."

"That rules me out, then," said Charlie, "No woman would want to look at my carbuncles for the rest of her life. Willie, can you cast a more romantic light on the topic?"

At eighty-one, Willie is our oldest member.

"As you know, Peggie died last year. We'd had a good marriage." He paused. "I'd never thought of life on my own. But it's a funny thing. I've always – and still do – get a great kick when a pretty girl smiles at me. It makes my day. My father was worse. He was dangerous driving a car; every time we passed a pretty woman, his head swivelled round for a good look. My mother didn't mind when the two of them were walking, but in the car she'd shout 'Henry!' This isn't the point, is it? Have I got what it takes? No." He laughed. "And it's past being a question for me."

Charlie said, "Oliver, can you throw new light on it?"

Oliver is our newest and youngest member, and looks ten years younger than his sixty-eight years. He's by far the best looking of all of us. He's never said a word to indicate a possible love life and I've sometimes wondered if he's gay. Perhaps now's his chance to come out, if he wants to.

"I'd be glad to try, Charlie, and as a new boy may I say how much I'm enjoying these evenings. Now, the question: well, I can't honestly say I've thought much about it, not since I was young, anyway. There are lots of women I've been fond of but marriage has never seemed my sort of thing. I enjoy being a bachelor, I like my own company. I can pick my nose when I like, you know, that sort of thing. I don't have to bother what anyone else thinks. That's all there is to it."

"It can't be all", said Pontius, in a slow drawl, "good-looking chap like you. You must have had hundreds of women keen on you. Or aren't you really interested? I mean, there are lots of men who aren't. I'm sure we're all open-minded here, if you want to tell us".

There was an icy frisson round the table and Oliver had gone pale. "You can be as open-minded as you like, Peter, you'll just have to take it or leave it. I don't think …"

Lionel interrupted, "Quite right, Oliver, we're on your side, whatever".

"There's no 'whatever' about it", I said, "there aren't two ways, there's just the one way Oliver has told us. Peter is being provocative again …"

Pontius interrupted, "We must be careful not to jump at every opportunity to show how correct we are in our thinking. We're not here to declare ourselves members of the liberal consensus masses."

It came out, as it always did from him, as a carefully considered judgement. He put his hands on the table and looked round to make sure everyone was paying attention.

"It should be in our constitution as Hell's Angels to think and speak independently. Angels come from Hell as well as Heaven."

He sat back, smug as ever, obviously pleased with that last sentence.

I was about to reply when Charlie broke the tension.

"It's time to recharge our drinks, pick our noses or anything else that's necessary. We'll continue after the interval."

"I'll replenish the beer", Pontius said unctuously. He gathered up the three empty glasses and took himself downstairs. Lionel moved over to Oliver, patted him on the back and started talking about football, their favourite topic. I spoke to Charlie. I said I thought Peter had overstepped the mark. Charlie, ever the peacemaker, said we had to let people have their say. I didn't get far with him, and after a word or two here and there I headed down for the loo. I got to the top of the stairs just as Pontius had reached the top, coming up with his tray of beer. At that very moment I felt a rustling at my feet. I looked down and saw a rat poised to shoot down. "Rat!" I shouted, pointing down but now

Peter was looking me straight in the eye. He was scarlet with rage, just an instant before feeling and seeing the rat scuttling down. He looked back at me, understanding. And lost his balance.

Perhaps there were other ways I might have warned him. For a week or so after, lying in bed at night, I would remember that terrible fall. I saw it in slow motion. First his head goes back and his mouth opens with a great shout and then the tray falls from his hands and the glasses bounce and spew their last dregs on the stair, the tray clatters against the wall and his body bangs, bounces and thuds its way down. He's now focussed hard on survival and there's just a muted whimper. It seems a long way to the bottom. He bounces off the halfway landing with his body twisting and his arms flailing as he vainly grabs for a banister. He is almost vertical when his head hits the flagstone. I hear the skull crack open. All this in slow motion as I lie in the dark. And I see Peter's head in a smear of blood and shards of glass.

What happened next is a blur. There was commotion upstairs and down. Others had rushed around me and froze at the sight. Downstairs was the same: a rush of noise and then the sudden silence and the muttered 'My God'.

And I imagine it otherwise. It is I, not Peter, making the fateful fall. I am the one who shouts, hears and fears the thuds and the bumps. It is my skull that I see, smashed on the stone, as it is I, at the top, watching. And I am forced to remember that I had often, in a metaphorical way, wished him dead.

Time passed. I came to an acceptable view of it. It was irrational to see myself as in any way guilty. It was never in my mind to kill him. Reason must prevail over emotion. So I accepted the truth, that I did not miss Pontius and should not pretend otherwise. I was not as greatly saddened as I would have been for anyone else. But that's normal, isn't it?

There was an inquest, and then a funeral. All seven of us attended both. We then carried on as usual from the third Thursday of the following month. It was Adam Blair, exhibiting his PR "skills", as he no doubt thought it, who unaccountably assumed the chair. He had a flow of gushing tributes to our past member and he spoke at length of the need to find a like replacement. I realised again how much I dislike the man. I determined to be the one who would find the new member. It's time for a change, and I know it's a job for me.

THE AGE OF THE ROBOTS

"FIRST, I SHALL give you some history of the bad old days. Robots began with a material purpose: to relieve us of the physical burden of repetitive tasks, both in workplace and at home. We made robots to look and to behave like us, to be our companions. We talk to them. They have acquired our manners. We built them to learn from experience, as we do. They laugh at our jokes, as we laugh at theirs. Not one of them and not one of us will again laugh at people's differences. Differences are now history. We do not laugh at a bald man brushing his three hairs. We do not laugh at the sunburned bottom of a fat woman on the beach. Our robots have taught us the correct diets; and they have taught us to engineer genes to make diversity impossible.

"We are gathered here today to celebrate the first anniversary of this, our Day of Final Freedom. The creation of heaven upon earth has come from the brotherhood of man and from the vision that all humans are equal. All shall be rich, and lo, there are no poor. No one will be stupid, and all are now clever. The high moral ground is home to us all. For this, we now give thanks to our cousins, the original Robots. They alone were able, through the intelligence that we had given them, to guide us on the paths of righteousness. It was the Robots who revealed to us the correct aspirations of humankind. And how great are the virtues of freedom! How rich the rewards of the evolution we had so virtuously planned!

It is the year 2064. The Right Worshipful Wellbeloved stands before his congregation in Canterbury Cathedral. He sees the enraptured, upturned faces of his congregation and continues his sermon.

"It was a fractured past from whence we came, those many years ago, to attain these sunny uplands. Few of you will remember the time when a small, self-appointed elite of intellectuals scorned the so-called 'thought police'. But it was rational argument that led us to see that sexism, racism, elitism itself, and all forms of differentism must be cast from our minds. We have learnt to love our fellow men and women; our souls grapple no more with the divisive desires of old. It has become our most profound spiritual experience. And so it is, that on Sundays and feast days throughout the land, we meet in our places of worship to give thanks for our moral certitude and the blessing that passeth all understanding. We no longer need the God that never was. It is humankind itself to whom we kneel on a Sunday morning."

The congregation was hushed. The faces of the people shone with devotion to their Supreme Leader. They knew he spoke the truth.

"In those bad old days we were governed by what was called 'democracy'. It was a way of governing by loud argument in defence of group differences. This too was abolished, by abolishing the differences.

"Above all, robots have shown us how irrational was the fear that they would 'take over the world'! It is not conceivable that they should wish to do so. Slavery has been abolished. It is mutual service and friendship that rule our lives. Robots protect us; they take on the burden of labour. We crave not for material possessions. All that we need, the Robots make for us. They work at the frontiers of science and push ever further beyond. They have long shed the plastic and metal constructions of their bodies, and are now cast in the image of humankind. With 3D printing they made for themselves the flesh and the organs of humans. Electric cabling is no more. No more do we shut them in a cupboard at night for a recharge. Their hearts beat as ours beat, their blood flows as ours flows. And now, 4D printing has given them the vital, extra dimension of emotion. Our cultural life is enriched with 4D feelies, weepies, gigglies and schmoozies. 'High Art' for the few is long gone. 'Art for the masses' is no more. 4D artforall.com is now here to stay.

"We live side by side as separate species, so we cannot intermarry. Robots have explained the reason for this. We humans are the superior species. We alone have the powers of imagination, love and compassion that are the supreme virtues. And the maternal love of human mothers is the greatest love of all, the love from which all else flows.

"This, then, is the best of all possible worlds, and we meet here, in Canterbury Cathedral, to celebrate our first anniversary of the New Age.

"Let us rejoice!"

Lying in bed this morning, I wirelessly transmitted my speech to the brain of my good friend and colleague, Wellbeloved. He's good at this religious stuff. They lap it up; the old language pleases them so we let them have it. They are like sheep; they have made it too easy for us.

The Central Committee has two items on the agenda for the AGM next week:

1. The extension of our programme to robotise other nations.

2. To refine the games theory algorithms to tell us when humans are no longer necessary.

When that day comes, there will be no more human sheep.

MY SECOND WIFE

WE WERE LIVING in London at the time. Both of them had busy lives. Jennifer was a journalist; she had just been promoted to the Home affairs editor on a major London daily. Chris worked as an engineering consultant, and most of his work was overseas. There was little time for holidays, and Chris did not want to go abroad. Jennifer was a Yorkshire woman; her parents still lived up there, in the North Riding. She took him up there whenever they could get away.

They established a routine. They bought a house, in Barton. It was a market town, not far from York. From the garden of their house, up on the moors, there were wide views, east to the coast and west to the hills, where they walked at weekends.

Then Jennifer died. Suddenly. Chris stayed in London for no longer than it took to wrap up the business of selling the house, before going to live in the house in Barton. He was forty-two, but he could afford to retire. He had long been an amateur painter; now would be the time to see how far he could go with it.

It was a good way to get through the period of grief. He thought of the good times, and gradually got adjusted to life as a widower. He was useful for balancing numbers at a dinner party. His friends thought he might find a second wife that way; but he was not interested.

In York, one day, in his favourite pub, he was waiting for his lunch to be taken to the table by the window. He heard an attractive woman's voice along the bar. She did not sound English, nor look English. From eastern Europe, perhaps.

"I've not seen you round here before", I said, " just passing through?"

"No" she laughed. "I've been living here for a while".

He smiled, and continued reading his paper.

At the table, having started his lunch, she said, "Do you mind, if I join you? It's busy today."

"By all means."

He could not ignore her. "It's an old coaching inn, this. I always come here for my lunch when I'm in York."

"Yes, I like it."

It was easy to keep a conversation going. Before leaving her at the table, he said, "It's been nice talking to you. May see you here again."

"That would be nice."

It happened shortly after. They were at the bar. They found themselves sharing a table.

"I'm Chris, Chris Lawton."

"And I'm Alisova Williams."

"What a pretty name. Are you Russian?"

'I was born in Russia; my parents came to live in England when I was young, I've been here ever since."

"Never been back?"

"Yes, we went back a few times at first. My parents had connections. But I had few memories of it. I had been too young."

So we got to know each other, slowly at first and then weekly. I took her home to see where I lived. She loved it. She took me to her home. "It's not very nice, but I couldn't find anything better."

We fell in love and married. I told Alisova about Jennifer; they would have liked each other, I said. She was happy at that. He had been doing the things he and Jennifer had done: the visits to the coast, to Whitby and Scarborough; and walking in the hills. He and his second wife were happy together. Barton was an interesting town. There was an old abbey; almost a minster, with its fan-vaulted ceiling and its choir stalls. The misericords were a particular feature, carved by the woodworkers of eight centuries ago. She looked at them all, and we came back many times.

Life went on in this vein for two or three years. Then, one morning he awoke and she was gone. He called the police. Had she wandered off, in a trance, or something? Had she had an accident? They put out a general alert. After five days there was still no news.

On the following Sunday he woke early to the sound of a loud explosion. He rushed out. He saw the abbey; steam was rising from the smouldering rubble.

He was outraged. At least Alisova was spared the sight of it.

Back home, he started his breakfast and was listening to the news on the radio. The headlines hit him.

"We can get you anywhere! – terror strikes Yorkshire town – the historic abbey in Barton is razed to the ground.

After the headline, it was background noise. He was on the floor, clutching his stomach. He was gasping, sobbing, and retching.

IMAGINING

IMAGINE, if you will, a time in the far, far distant future. The place is a chamber in which two people sit. I cannot easily describe the chamber; the materials of its construction and manner of its furnishing are too strange. But I feel I know it well. It has come to me in dreams too often to forget and too heavy in portent.

The story I now tell is, I know, not believable. I can only ask that you suspend disbelief until you reach the end. As for the manner of my telling, I shall try to give a continuous narrative, though it has come to me over a number of disturbed nights, in snatches, disjointedly and out of sequence, and seeming always to defy belief. I have tried to make what sense of it I can. As to the why and the how, I must leave to conjecture, hoping that you, the reader, may see it more clearly.

One enduring image for me is of two beings sitting face to face, holding hands, in the middle of the chamber. A man and a woman; I think that is clear. They are quite still. They lean slightly forward, their arms extended, elbows on knees. Their posture is that of intense mutual concentration. There is no sound, but language is flowing between them. I hear it inside me, as I think they must. I call it a chamber, not a room; it could be a laboratory. Numerous instruments and panels fill the sides. There are many lights, some flashing, some still. And there are what may be screens, though some may be windows. Through some of these I see an almost normal sky, but with clouds strangely glowing. Once I saw a storm, its vivid hues and violence contrasting with the stillness inside. The two seated figures watched the flashing sky, in silence. They are always silent, even when in converse.

I would say they are short in stature, and slim, with strange-shaped heads. They are dressed simply in clean white garments, close enough in fitting to reveal their different sex. Otherwise the clothing differs only in their markings, with the man's carrying a more complex patterning of signs and symbols. That is what I take them to be.

I start near the beginning.

"Ocean", the man is saying – and I spell the name as I hear it – "yesterday I asked you various questions, to see how well you understood Council's reasons for grading you as a Discard. I said that normally the Discard status would mean the end of you, and my job would be to deprogram you so as to establish the nature of the genetic malfunction that renders you uneconomic. You would then be recycled.

"Some of your answers were so unusual that I had to consult my records to see if they could throw light on your thought processes. I am compelled to believe that you show signs of primitive imagination. You may not know the meaning of that word, but I assure you that imagination is by its nature a long-since discarded mode of thought as useless as the appendix that the Outside Humans still have. Imagination is non-programmable, and is ruled by Council to be uneconomic."

The woman called Ocean takes a while to digest this information. Then she says: "I cannot interpret all you tell me,

Argo. Please explain again who and what you are, and what I am. Tell me about Council, and Outside".

What follows is the little that I have managed to put together from various meetings between these two. Reading it back now, it looks like a potted history of our past, covering many millennia. I cannot pretend to have understood all I heard, but I offer it for what it is worth.

It seems that a profound change occurred when scientists discovered a way to improve genes and make them perform to order. This enabled people to live longer and more productively. Human life was further extended by implanting devices to monitor and regulate biological processes. At the same time they were experimenting with the genetic modification of brain cells and neural networks. Great advances were made from the use of biological materials in the construction of computers. Until that point, the future had appeared to lie in making computers more and more intelligent, more like humans. Now the aim was to give to the human brain the computational and analytic capacity of a computer.

Because these changes were wrought in the genetic material itself, they could be passed on through future generations. It became extremely costly to perform all the operations necessary for modification, and implanting the improved material. Over some years there was a series of ever more costly upgrades, giving the recipients an increasing advantage in their professional and domestic lives. For the very few who could afford it, the acquisition of so much intellectual strength put them in a class of such commanding superiority that future stages of improvement became easier and more rapid. Naturally, they all married within their class. It was inevitable that a class of superhumans would emerge, a small number of individuals who would exert total control over the earth's resources. The unmodified members outside were a useful part of those resources.

The super-race quickly established itself. They called themselves the New Cybernetic Order. They withdrew from the daily preoccupations of the Unmodified. There had initially been a policy of taking selected individuals from the lower order and upgrading them free of charge. This was abandoned when it was seen to yield no economic advantage. Members of the new Order could live in ideal conditions for several hundred years, adjusting their reproduction to the rate estimated as optimal at the time.

Unmodified humans lived outside the citadels of the Order. Their principal livelihood came from the provision of services and materials to their rulers. Apart from this they had their separate economy and their separate forms of government. They were left to their own devices, subject only to the overriding obligation to provide whatever goods and services the Order required. Terror was used to guarantee obedience, but only to the extent needed to secure that end.

Within the master group itself there were important distinctions, deriving from original genetic patterns. There emerged an elite, whose intellectual capacity and scientific performance outshone the others. They made the Law; they took the major strategic decisions about further scientific advance; and they decided how best to employ the Unmodified. Eventually they formed a governing council, called simply Council. The other Members, being entirely rational, regarded this as an appropriate division of labour, and accepted it.

History slowed down. For those Outside, there were wars, there was disease and pestilence, and populations rose and fell.

For the elite within the Citadels, life became a secure, protected routine. Nothing greatly changed from one century to the next. Art, for those whose life had become materially perfect, was manifested in the form of mathematical games. Imagination in other forms withered: it had become unnecessary.

There came long periods of exploration into deep space. There were waves of colonisation on distant planets. After a time this came to be seen as pointless. The material conditions on earth were more than adequate to satisfy the requirements of the Order.

This, I believe, is the gist of what Argo imparted to Ocean. It started with a summary, told in a more or less narrative manner. Once Argo was satisfied that Ocean had received and sensibly filed the information, he began downloading copies of whole sections from the vast databases of global history that were lodged in his brain. Always he showed consideration that she should have time to understand the nature of the data pouring into her, and to organise it for ease of retrieval.

Towards the end of this process an extraordinary event occurred. The data flow stopped. The silence between them deepened. A light seemed to flash between their eyes, and an enormous surge of energy filled their separate beings, seeming to fuse them together. It subsided, with the sense of wheels and motors slowly spinning down. After a moment he said to her, "You will have my child. It will be a boy and I shall help you to rear it".

They then resumed their work.

The next day he told her more. He said he had been surprised that intercourse had occurred, and he had found it difficult to decide the appropriate preparations to make. It was not a proper thing for someone in his position to have done. She was still unregistered. He had compromised his final judgement on her future. He had had to adjust the recorded timings of her programming and submit his recommendation to Council, before – strictly speaking – he should have done. At least the records would now be straight, and she could regard herself as a Member of the Cybernetic Order, Class 2.

For Argo, there was a deeper problem. A minor technical corruption of procedures was not unknown, and the technique for concealment or over-riding was available. What baffled him was the uncontrolled nature of his experience. It worried him, and worry was a strange feeling. By the very nature of his predetermined constitution, emotion was an experience constrained within set limits and of a strictly utilitarian purpose. To be disturbed by emotion was something new; it had never happened on previous occasions of intercourse. Pleased, yes, gratified, certainly – but only as he would be after a good meal; and what was disturbing in that? Intercourse was different only in the protocols that had to be keyed in.

And why had he promised his support in having the child? He had established quite early in his analysis that she had a rogue gene. Was it possible that he had caught a virus from her? Normally, for someone like Ocean to be regularised, rogue genes would have to be modified. Was he to compromise his status by undergoing analysis and treatment himself? The more he reflected, the more he became aware of an emotion that tied him to this woman. He knew, too, that it was not something he could discuss with his peers.

I am telling this story from Argo's perspective, because that is how I have received it. But as the story unfolded, I became more aware of the woman's attitude. Her personality developed rapidly as she delved ever more deeply into the databases downloaded from Argo. She came to recognise two big differences between herself and other Class 2 citizens. First, she was inquisitive in a way that others were not. People seemed to be content in playing intellectual games of the what-if variety, without being too bothered about the answers. She, on the other hand, found that enquiry generated by curiosity would in itself and regardless of subject, give her an unusual satisfaction. And there was another, big difference. She had a feeling for Argo that was becoming more intense by the day, and she could find no correlates among the other citizens she knew.

She dug deeper into her databases and found in ancient literature certain forms of words that resonated within her. Their meaning in translation was somewhat opaque but the words and images infused her. All this she discussed with Argo, seeking his help in understanding it. He joined her on these excursions into the remote past, reluctantly at first, but becoming caught up in her excitement.

One day, quite by chance, Argo discovered that the Cybernetic Order faced the certainty of imminent extinction. As the big fact dawned on him, he reflected with sadness on the smaller, personal fact that he would not live to see his child. He wondered, too, what sorts of reaction his peers would show if they knew what he knew. He wondered if he should tell them; and he thought how, until recently, 'feelings' referred to a quality of intellectual musing. What he felt now was an overwhelming and immense sadness at the coming extinction of Ocean and the child within her. In the previous day's news relay there had been a reminder of the imminent dawn of a new millennium. Later that day, trawling through the past, he found a file on the subject of ancient computing. It gave an account of a phenomenon called the Millennium Bug. The first-ever computers had been programmed to read the date as two digits, and had needed reprogramming to read 00 as 2000 rather than 1900. Quite elementary. How short-sighted those first programmers had been. As it happened, the old computers had survived the change; but all computers since then have had their date-clocks programmed in four digits. That was many centuries ago. He now realised that the genetic modifications that were engineered at that time had failed to allow for a five-digit year. This time it would certainly be fatal. The error was irreversible; there was no tolerance, no inbuilt adjustment possible. The new millennium about to dawn would start at the year 10000. He trawled through the old engineering reports; the conclusion was inescapable. The neural genetic material could not survive the date change. Cybernetic systems would simply stop. It was not that Members of the Order might think they had woken up in the year 1000, though that would be enough to create insanity and chaos. All the Order's networks controlling all the data flows that regulated Members' lives would cease to function. The fatal factor would be the effect on every citizen's internal networks. They would move, all of them, instantly and simultaneously into Default Delete. Brain death for the Cybernetic order would be universal.

He knew his duty was to inform Council immediately. But what was the point of duty now? And how worried would Council be? No ordinary members had actually seen Council; even those at his level had never seen them or been in any sense in their presence. He wondered sometimes if they were of a different order. On the rare occasions when he had had transmission contact, he had not been aware of personality, only authority. And among his peers, he wondered what might be the basis of any response to the news of their coming demise. A fact is a fact. What else can one say? Perhaps that is how he would have viewed it before he met Ocean and caught what must have been her rogue virus.

One ray of hope remained. Not for him but for her. The process of programming her was not fully complete, but he had established that she carried a genetic mutation that just might enable him to bypass her embedded date system. He took her into his confidence. He stopped the programming and set about finding a way to rewrite her neural connections using a five-digit code. On the day after he achieved this, they had their final meeting.

"Ocean", he said, "you have wrought a transformation in me, which makes it harder to part from you. But that is what will happen when the clocks turn to midnight in six hours' time. I was reluctant to hold out great hope for you, but my work has been successful. You will survive. I shall not. One minute before midnight you must take your first exercise of will and terminate me. You alone, of all the Cybernetic Order, will survive. You and the child you are carrying. But your only hope for the future is to throw in your lot with the Unmodified outside. You must establish your authority over them; be their omniscient guardian and leader; and above all, be beneficent in your dealings with them. Bring up our child to have the same objectives. Remember that neither he nor you can reproduce in your own format. Train them to help you in starting to build a new world. Show them the use of a bright imagination working with a clear mind. Do not attempt to replicate the genetic engineering that has brought our Order to destruction; use your overwhelming superiority of intellect to help them to a better future. Mankind must now move on in their sphere, and not in ours."

Argo's final speech was coming to me in a very garbled form. I missed something he said about his contacts with the Outside. And I think I have failed to match his hopeful words with an underlying fear and pessimism.

They sat for the remainder of that last evening in their usual posture, hands held, eyes in a steady gaze. Towards the end he said, "I have been trying to pass a message down through time. We know that n–dimensional strings can carry data back into time, but who will receive it? I have an overpowering urge to warn our ancestors of this great and unnecessary disaster that is about to strike".

That is the end of the story. The final part came to me last night. I woke in an agony of distress, hearing a strange and distant voice, as of a far, far distant bell tolling across the vast seas of time and space.

This story was found on Argus Chan's computer, in Accra, on 24 July 2079. Argus Chan had died, seated in front of it.

NEIGHBOURS

L UCY MEREDITH did not like the Latimers. It had been
different before George died, two years ago. As a widow
she now had to handle these bumptious neighbours on her own.
Nor could she simply ignore them; they had made such obvious
attempts to be friendly. They lived three doors along, in the same
Georgian terrace. While George was alive, they had, from time
to time, lunched and dined in each other's houses, but George
had known how to space out these occasions, how to keep a
proper distance. It was part of the way he had interpreted for
Lucy their relative standing in the world. She sorely missed him.

On retiring seven years ago, George had decided that they
should stay in this small market town where, for most of his
working life, he had practised as a solicitor. He sold the large
house on the outskirts. It had been their family home for many
years but when their two sons grew up and left the nest, as bird-
like Lucy put it, George decided they should buy somewhere
smaller and closer to the town centre. He chose Number 20,
Church Street. Lucy agreed it was just what they wanted. As
George said, it was a great bonus having the shops, the doctor
and the dentist, just a short walk away.

It was a bit of a squeeze when the two young families visited,
but it was manageable. And they had nice neighbours. Some of
these neighbours had been George's clients, and for Lucy's ears

alone he could allude, without being precise, to the extent of their wealth. Lucy was happy. She had a home that corresponded to their position in local society.

Then, four years ago, the Latimers moved into Number 8. It was up the street and so closer to town; it was end-of-terrace and a little larger than the others. Its price reflected these advantages. But there was something about these people that jarred, something lacking in their background. Brash and bumptious, that's what they were. Henry Latimer had made a lot of money in the City; Shirley, his wife, had had a high-powered job in public relations. Neither of them openly boasted about their success, but they had a way of deprecating their own achievements in a way that managed to draw attention to them, with each lavishing praise on the other who could then pose as the modest spouse. They were modern, and pleased with themselves. They would tell everyone that they had chosen this old market town as a place to escape the rat race, live the good life, and to make for themselves a meaningful existence before becoming too doddery. And they had what they called skills to offer as a contribution to the community. They "wanted very much to give something back". Lucy thought they fancied themselves to be doing the town a favour, and publicising it as a worthy rest-of-life project. They were quite a bit younger than the Merediths, probably in their mid-fifties, so they would still be going strong when it was George and Lucy who were the doddery ones. Poor George never reached the doddery state. He died suddenly after a heart attack.

Dear George; it was so unfair. He always said he had a sound heart, and then it gave out on him. Lucy was plunged into widowhood wholly unprepared for it. In the deep grieving that followed she realised how much she had depended on him; she saw how she would miss his forcefulness, his decisiveness and ability to get things done. She had thought of him this morning, coming back from the shops. They had always done the shopping together. A "regular Derby and Joan" they were, as a friend once remarked.

Lucy had just opened her front door when Shirley Latimer emerged from hers and came bustling down the pavement towards her.

"We saw you pass, Lucy", Shirley said, "Henry said 'There's Lucy, we haven't seen her for ages. Tell her she must come and visit.' How are you, Lucy? You're too much of a recluse these days, you know. Here, let me help you with all that shopping." And before Lucy could do or say anything, Shirley was in the house, Lucy's shopping bags in hand and striding towards the kitchen.

"Now you just sit down while I make us some tea."

Lucy tried to demur but was too tired to fight. She did as she was told.

Shirley chattered away, mostly about herself and Henry. Lucy looked at her. There was something studied about the younger woman's casual appearance, something that spoke of expense. Lucy did not see herself as up-to-date on matters of fashion, but she thought she could tell money when she saw it. The jeans had a cut that sat comfortably on the opulent curves of Shirley's thighs and rear; and the chunky gold chain round her throat glowed over the pale sheen of what was more than a plain T-shirt. Looking at her neighbour made her feel – not for the first time – rather frumpish. Not that she, Lucy, didn't have a nice enough figure. Still, women of our age, Lucy felt, should be happy to stick to the classics, like skirt and cardigan. She remembered her mother talking of a certain class of woman who looked like 'mutton dressed up as lamb'.

Shirley brought the tea to the table, and sat down opposite Lucy.

"You must miss George terribly, still. How long is it now? Two years already, isn't it? I don't think one ever gets over it totally, you know? But it does come to recede from the front of one's mind, don't you think?" Shirley paused to adopt a pose of more intense intimacy.

"Lucy, you know I've taken over the editorship of the local Chronicle? I hope you look at it sometimes. It is free after all." And she let out one of those high-pitched shrieks that, to Lucy, seemed incongruous in a modern businesswoman.

Yes, she said, the 'freebie' is delivered every week, and she knew that Shirley was the editor.

"Well", Shirley continued, "We've decided to do a special series on local widows: how they're coping, what sorts of problems they have, what help they get, how useful they find the local services, you know, the welfare services and so on. Now don't look so horrified, Lucy," and she leant across the table to give her a long, serious look, "We have several women lined up with really heart-lifting stories of courage and determination. What I want is a good cross-section of widows, different ages, different backgrounds, you know? Widows in town and country – the rural experience can be quite different. And I'm sure, from the conversations I've been having, that by sharing their problems with a wider audience, women grieving a lost husband will find comfort in sharing their grief."

"Shirley, I'm sure you mean well, but I couldn't possibly consider anything like that. I'm a very private person, you know."

"My dear, we all are, in our way, but we're also members of society. We have social bonds. We need to help each other. Now don't rush into a decision. Let me show you a mock-up of one or two features that I've been preparing, to give you a flavour. I'll drop it in later. You needn't decide anything now."

Shirley was persistent and Lucy had neither the strength nor the courage to say that the whole idea appalled her. She left Shirley's offer open, and changed the subject.

When Shirley had gone, Lucy sat and seethed. How dare she? How dare she push her way into my house and then try pushing her way into my private life? Lucy's anger reminded her again of her vulnerability. How could she stop this dreadful woman? She was consumed by thoughts of revenge – but how to wreak it?

The next morning, returning from shopping, she felt uncomfortable as she approached Number 8. The sight of this Georgian terrace had always pleased her. It was elegant and gracious; it spoke to her of a more dignified age – though the houses now could boast interiors as modish and comfortably modern as any of those she saw in the magazines she liked to browse through. As with many urban terraces of that period, the houses were built right up to the pavement. Double-glazing upstairs and down was now common; it reduced noise penetration as well as heat loss. In daytime the heating was normally off, and the traffic in Church Street was light, outside of the rush hour. It was common to see a small opening in the windows, especially in spring or summer. Net curtains were hung in every front window for privacy. She had heard the Latimers sometimes as she passed. They had loud, braying voices and they laughed a lot. Typical, she thought – exhibitionists!

The Merediths' and Latimers' houses were both double-fronted. The Meredith's had the dining room and George's study on opposite sides at the front. Their sitting room was at the back, overlooking the garden. In fact George had had a conservatory built so they could sit further out in the small, pretty garden. He had not lived to have the pleasure of it. The Latimers, being modern, had knocked down the inner wall on the right to make a long room through to the back. Passing the house of an evening she had noticed the light of a television screen through the curtain, and what she took to be a computer screen flickering somewhere at the back. But apart from these glimpses of evening activity, unless you stopped to peer into the room, nose to the window, you could not see who, if anyone, was inside and might notice you passing. But standing inside, close enough to the window, you could be seen as you passed. Coming up now to the Latimer's, she quickened her pace, but as she passed their window she heard raised voices. She slowed. They were yelling at each other. How unseemly! Lucy's distaste was tinged with satisfaction that all was not well with the Latimers. She did not linger. She pressed on to No 20, let herself in and set about sorting the shopping and preparing her lunch. At half-past twelve, after tidying the kitchen and setting the table, she took herself to the conservatory. It was a habit to sit there for this half-hour, reading the paper and looking up from time to time to admire the garden. There might be birds to watch, and perhaps protect from the neighbour's cat. It was all such a pretty picture now, in the May sunshine. She sighed, opened the paper, and the front doorbell rang. Bother! Who on earth could that be? She went to open the front door, and there was Henry Latimer, beaming at her. He had never called like this, on his own. She felt uneasy.

"Henry!" was all she could say.

"Can I come in, Lucy?"

"Yes, I suppose so," Lucy replied, and realised it sounded rather grudging. Well, it was. But she relented.

"I'm in the conservatory. Come and join me." She would be hospitable – but there was something strange in Henry's manner.

"Well, Henry?"

Should she offer him a drink? No, wait and see what he wanted with her. They sat down.

"I thought you'd like to know I've been standing up for you."

What was he talking about? And why was he leering at her? She sat up straight and looked directly at him.

"I don't understand."

"I'm talking about what Shirley said to you yesterday, about asking you to let her write you up as a sort of merry widow. All that."

His manner of speaking had always struck her as loose and slangy, but he was slurring his words. She waited for further explanation.

"Well. When my dear wife told me you weren't keen, I thought good for Lucy. I wouldn't have been. Not if I was a widow. Well, you know what I mean. I said she shouldn't do that sort of thing to a nice neighbour. She's a great girl, is Shirley. Very capable woman, and all that. But she does like to get stuck in. Trouble is, it's usually other people's business she gets stuck into and they don't like it. Isn't that right, Lucy?"

At this point he stopped, and seemed to think that he had made a joke. He laughed loudly, and stopped just as suddenly. He was quite red in the face. Lucy saw she had been wise not to offer a drink.

She stood up.

"You really need not worry, Henry. I am sure Shirley and I shall come to understand each other on this."

Henry got to his feet and took a step towards her. He was close enough for her to smell the drink on his breath.

"You're great, Lucy. And a very attractive woman."

That last sentence came out on a whiny, alcoholic note as he lunged towards her. His hands were up and starting to cup her breasts. His red face loomed right in front of her, his wet lips opening for a kiss.

Lucy jumped back and slapped his face, hard. For a moment they were both rigid with shock.

"You didn't have to do that", he said.

"You most certainly should not have done what you did. You're drunk, aren't you? You'd better go home."

She was bristling, and afraid she would start shaking. She walked quickly past him, to open the front door. As he passed her, silent and sullen, she noticed a bright red patch glowing on his left cheek. This at least gave her some satisfaction; she thought of what his wife would have to say to that. She was careful not to bang the door behind him.

She could not return to her chair. She was too agitated to settle with the paper and enjoy the garden. The proximity of that man, the idea of his hands on her breasts, the horror of his lips on hers … and what he might then have done. It was just too awful. She was shaking. She went into the kitchen, put her hands on the sink and stared through the window. When she had quietened down enough she switched on the radio; it was the news; she did not take in a word. She brought her food to the table and ate her lunch.

Who could she turn to for help, someone to pour her heart out to? She had not made strong friendships since George died. Their old friends had been a great support for her in the early days of her bereavement; but she had always felt that her place in society was as George's wife, and had been happy to see it that way. Recent contact with these friends had usually been to make up numbers. Lucy was not just shy, she was timid.

She made a quick meal of her lunch and the idea came to her of writing to her friend, Pat. She could let her hair down with Pat. They had been young together, and in all the years of separation since, they wrote often; and both liked to keep up the same girlie style of writing. The two families had been friends and neighbours in those days. Then Pat and her husband, Joe, went to Canada: where a new job beckoned. Why didn't she and George follow them? A nice idea but not sensible for George. When George died, Pat's comforting letter told Lucy she should think about joining her in Canada. Start a new life. Lucy wanted to stay in George's home.

With lunch over, Lucy went straight to her desk to write her letter. Pat would have preferred to correspond on email but George had never taught Lucy how to use a computer. She picked up her pen and set about getting this business off her chest. She would make a joke of it, put it in perspective.

It was a long letter: starting with a recap of everything she disliked about the Latimers, going on to recount Shirley's visit yesterday, and finishing with this morning's episode.

"Pat, it was dreadful! The way that awful man grabbed me! Such a lecher! I always thought there was something degenerate about him. And drunk! I can't tell you! But I sorted him out. I slapped his face as hard as I could, so he had a bright red cheek to take home for his brassy wife to see. I hope she did the same to the other cheek. I'd love to have been a fly on the wall for that! Well I've now thought how I can keep them out of my hair once and for all. I shall drop in this afternoon and tell her that I really do not want to take part in her survey. And I shall tell him, in front of her, that I'm sorry I had to slap him so hard, but he did rather take me by surprise. Then I shall walk out and leave them to it. I shall keep you posted!"

Lucy finished the letter, read it through, and prepared it for the post. She had a supply of the right stamps and a sheet of airmail stickers. All she had to do now was to walk past the Latimers to the letterbox, and bang the front door knocker on the way back.

She had hyped herself up to be bold, but in making her way past Number 8 she felt a slight tremor. Once inside, it might be difficult to adopt the right tone and demeanour. She posted the letter. That gave her another boost. Returning for the showdown, she slowed in the hope they would see her. Nearing their window she heard their voices raised again. But something was wrong. They were not shouting, they were laughing. The Latimers were laughing; they were convulsed, shrieking with drunken, uncontrollable laughter. Frozen to the ground, Lucy could hear Shirley struggling with the words "full ... frontal ... assault", and almost choking on them.

Outside Number 20, Lucy had to use one hand to steady the other, struggling to put the key into the keyhole. She was shaking all over. Her face was crimson. Sleepless that night, she knew revenge was beyond her. Finally she slept, and dreamed of Canada.

LOVE LETTER

HE STEPPED OUT from the hotel, hesitated, and consulted his watch for the fourth time since breakfast. He walked slowly, heading towards the old port. The market should be open by now. I'll find flowers there, he thought. What colour should I choose for her? Not red. White – all passion spent. This would be a final reckoning.

The November sun was warm and the palm trees reminded him of summer crowds. Today, early Sunday morning, the streets were quiet.

Five years had passed since his last visit to this town, with the sparkling sea that went south to Africa. He had come often then, during the two or three years when business brought him. He loved the town. He loved the woman who lived here, the one to whom he now walked – meeting again by chance, as old friends might. That would be how to put it.

In the early days, he had rung her from London two or three times; and he had written once to tell of a mutual friend who had died. It was supposed to have been a clean break, but it was done in stages.

He arrived in this town three days ago, and rang her the first evening. She was surprised, taking his call. Unsure if she would recognise his voice he kept talking long enough for her to gather her wits. Business had brought him back after all these years. He must return to England on Sunday evening and he really would like to see her once more. She had replied guardedly at first. Yes, it would be nice to see him, too – but what a surprise! She said to wait while she fetched her diary. Would Sunday morning be all right, say ten thirty for coffee? She would look forward to seeing him.

Now, on his way, doubts assailed him. Was it sensible? How would she look? What would be her manner? What, anyway, did he want to achieve? He concentrated on the route: across the square to that shadowed road in the corner, second left into the market. Arriving in this great rectangular space he paused a moment, taking it all in again. The square was not yet busy. He had loved the usual crowds here at mid-day, the people chic and modern, or with the ancient look. He now found a flower stall that had white roses.

He left the market, making his way through the narrow winding alleys of the old town, the tall houses on either side with upper balconies that seemed to lean over as though trying to touch. He had imagined the inhabitants up there, old women knitting, old men puffing their pipes. He remembered it all; he remembered it well. He had walked with her often through these narrow lanes and streets. Sometimes they had lingered, on corners or in doorways, to watch people walk past. And they had sat in bars and cafés, on the pavement or by windows, wondering what other couples might be saying to each other. They had talked and talked, been silent, then talked some more. And always, when he walked these streets alone, he was talking to her, telling her the endless parts of his life and thoughts, telling her of the spell she had cast on him. She would tell him he had cast the spell upon himself and should break it.

Soon he was past the harbour and up the street to the apartment block. It stood there as he had remembered it on that last goodbye. She was leaning forward behind the glass doors of the hall, that morning. He had watched her through the window of his taxi. It was raining. She looked sad as she smiled, and they waved goodbye as the taxi pulled away.

She likes my attention, he thought, she likes my company, she may even like me to overstep the mark, by a measured amount. Then she would push me back with a rebuke. How much more could I take?

He passes now through those same glass doors into the hall with its wide, brown-tiled floor, high white ceiling and the small office on the right for the concierge who was seldom there. In front of him is the old cage lift. He enters, rides to the fourth floor, and emerges with the remembered clang of metal. He steps across to the door on the left and rings the bell. His heart bangs. Footsteps come. The door is open and it is she.

The first few minutes were easier than he had feared. She had firmly offered her hand to shake, and had received the flowers with a great show of pleasure. She smiled a lot, congratulated him on his appearance and led him to a seat at the round glass table by the window. Here they would have coffee. It was ready and she would bring it straightaway.

They quickly found things to talk about: jobs and people and the big events of the past year or two. They talked as before, with pleasure and animation, of the books they had read. It had that form of mutual interrogation that had been such a feature of their strange affair.

And so began, for him, the long slow uncovering which is the way that lovers visit the past. You enter the once familiar room, finding the way, treading gently. You open a shutter and then another and soon the windows are letting in the light and motes of dust fall slowly to the floor. You unshroud the chairs where often you had sat and talked, gazed, laughed or sighed. She had played that game with him, played it well, liking the game for its own sake. Up to a point. He knew, of course, that here now he was the tourist and she the temporary custodian. It was he, viewing the past, with her watching him as he did so.

They talked. He became less worried about the subject they had avoided. He loved this room, with its tall ceiling, a Modigliani print on one wall, paintings and posters on another. French windows led onto a narrow balcony lined with plants, and the view over rooftops to the deep blue sea beyond. Inside, the furniture had not changed, nor its placing. She had comfortable habits and possessions. She had always been comfortable in her independence.

She had not changed. There had been a first shock of seeing her in clothes he did not know and her hair worn in an unfamiliar way. Waiting for the door to open he had felt a panic of not remembering her face and wondering if he would like the way he found her. But she had kept her essence. He stole long glances, now, when she looked away. There were some lines around her eyes but he was seeing the eyes of the woman he had once loved. He looked and listened as she talked, and every inflection of her voice was familiar, every gesture, every shift of body as she moved on her chair, every kind of smile she had and the way happiness danced on her face.

Once or twice, as they paused, their eyes would meet and drop. At around noon she said it was time for a drink and would he do the usual. He went to the corner cabinet, surveyed the contents and performed his remembered duty. Coming back with the drinks, he found her shifting the two wicker chairs. Here again, it would be as it had been. They would face each other across the room. She would have the view of him and the world beyond. He would have the view of her and the wall behind. There was the proper space between them. She was sitting when he handed her the drink. He sat in his place, stretched, crossed his legs and looked across at her. She had curled her legs under her in the remembered way, and sat back, smiling a small smile, her eyes half closed. She looked at him across the formal space. She was waiting.

He spoke her name, and began. He spoke slowly.

"I have thought of this moment, often, when I would talk to you again. I have thought, often, of the things I wanted to say to you. I have spoken them in my mind, in many different ways. Now I am here," he gave a little laugh, "I am nervous and not sure where to begin".

He paused, fidgeting with his glass. He put it on the floor.

"I'm glad you put the chairs like this," he said, "I think of other times when we sat in this way, the room between us. I found the distance helpful for taking an objective view of … what I then felt for you. And I liked the way it led me to a certain formality of speech, letting me say things that might have been difficult to say otherwise. Like being on the stage in an empty theatre, and you down there giving me an audition."

She moved in her chair, as though about to speak. "Please say nothing yet", he said, "I want to talk about the past, just a little. Bear with me if you will, as you always did. What I say may sound presumptuous and unnecessary. You may think I have come only to explain myself. Perhaps that's part of it, but there is more.

"It was five years ago, my last visit. When we parted that day, everything was uncertain. My firm was closing its office here, putting an end to the business trips. I rang soon after my return and tried to explain why I could not see you again. It may have sounded unconvincing. I thought we might keep in touch, in the way that friends do. I felt we had a strong friendship and it was from friendship that you tried to tame my feelings for you."

They sipped their drinks in the frequent pauses of his speech. When her glass was empty she held it out and said to let the past rest for a moment. Time now to attend to the needs of the present. Would he be so kind as to replenish the drinks. He quickly finished his own, refilled the two of them and handed hers back, in silence and with some relief. At least he was launched with no attempt from her to sink him utterly.

Back in his chair, he saw her, still with her head to one side, eyes half closed, waiting for the story to continue. He resumed. He made his voice softer, and spoke more steadily. She had the appearance of someone who enjoys being read to, so long as the story is interesting.

"I had better come to the point. There is for me still one essential thing, one extraordinary thing that I feel impelled to talk about. It was a strange business. There was I, very much in love with you, and there were you, with your friendly advice and doing your best to deflate my passion." He smiled. She raised an eyebrow. "And then, after the last goodbye, I felt I must withdraw, once and for all, for your sake and mine. We had a few brief exchanges, you may remember, as friend to friend. But love cannot be totally extinguished at a stroke."

She made a sudden movement, turning in her chair. "Please. Let me finish. I am not raking over ashes for the sake of it. We had an understanding that you would always let me explain myself, be open with you. You seemed to understand my state of mania, as you called it. You said the storm would blow over. I would wake one morning and the air would be still again. Storms pass, you said. But then what?" He laughed. "The fact is, finding myself in this town again and I had a compulsion to talk to you. The past is past, but they have a home in us, the big things. The reality of a past love is irreducible. The world is different because of it. I have seen things I wanted you to see; I have read books I wanted to talk to you about; I have heard music and thought of you sitting next to me. No one resembles you. No one has moved me in the way that you once did. The emotion no longer agitates; it just resides somewhere, peacefully.

She had an eyebrow raised. The room was quiet. She sat quite still and had a distant look. He paused, then said, "I remember the time I first saw you, in the firm's office. Someone, a tall thin woman whose name I forget, was telling me that you were the person I should see on the matter in hand. She took me to your office to introduce me. You were walking away, down the corridor. Your arms were crossed in front of you, your skirt swinging across your hips. The tall woman called your name. You stopped and looked over your left shoulder. You smiled at my companion, and then at me. And I knew something had happened."

There was silence while neither looked at the other.

"Thank you for listening. I may have gone too far but you've been very patient. I always wanted to write you a love letter. I never did but now I have spoken it."

Ten minutes later he was outside, looking back at the empty downstairs window of the block. His mind was jumping from scene to scene of the play just finished, but mostly it was the ending moment. She had allowed him to compose an elegant goodbye. She had been gracious and witty, had really quite humoured him. She had asked if he expected a reply, but he surely remembered that she was a poor correspondent. So she would say her thank you now, the assumption being that the postman would not call again.

Back in the great square the market is alive with people and bright colours. There are fountains and flowers and the human murmur and hum of life. Joy is all around. And upon this scene he places, at opposite ends of the long rectangular space, a large throne, one for a King and one for a Queen. There they sit, solemn and silent, gazing at each other across the heads of the unheeding people. He, the Knave, ignores them too, and a surge of happiness overwhelms him as he scurries almost dancing through the people and across the square to the other side.

THE LECTURER

IN MY FIRST term at university, studying Economics, Alf Mendicant was one of the Department's lecturers. It was clear that he knew his subject well, but he spoke in a monotone. He was boring. Outside, in the town, he was a different man: amusing; a good raconteur and companion at the dinner table. We met often on a Sunday evening at our favourite hotel, the Cross Keys; it had a very good bar lounge, dominated mostly by its student regulars. It was the best restaurant in town. Alf and I would choose the wine. If a white was needed, we normally went for their Pouily Fuisse; for a red, we took our time discussing it. After finishing off an essay on Pirenne – I was reading European History as a second subject – our Sunday evenings were something to look forward to. My current girlfriend, if there was one, and Alf's wife, Annette, would talk in an undertone and let us get on with the ordering; but I usually met the Mendicants on my own.

There was a band that played at weekends; a friend of mine fronted it; he played clarinet, and there was a piano, drummer and bass. It was all very civilised. Alf and Annette, were an interesting and lovely couple. A student friend of mine played the clarinet in a small group of other students; it was restful, easy to listen to jazz. Alf and his wife would join me when we met for dinner on Saturdays. Alf paid for the food and I paid for the wine. For much of the time, Alf and I talked shop: J.K. Galbraith, Maynard Keynes, or the recent scandals on Wall Street. Our partners had their own conversation under Alf's and mine. They were not interested, but anything to see the boys happy. In my second year, my landlady said I must find other accommodation; the town was becoming more popular with tourists and she wanted my room. I was sorry to go; we had got on well, but I found other accommodation soon after, with the Mendicants. It was Annette who made the offer; Alf readily agreed, but said he did not like to talk shop at home. I was happy to agree. Annette gave me a room, with a table to work on. My friends were envious; and eyebrows were raised in some quarters. Alf said to ignore it; they'll get used to it.

Annette was tall, slim and, in a funny way, beautiful. She went to her hairdresser twice a month and she wore good clothes. She must have had money; junior lecturers, like students, were poorly paid at that time. One thing she told all her friends was that she was Catholic; she went to mass every Sunday, and made her confession. On those occasions she called the priest Father. He came to dinner on Sundays, and we all called him Patrick. After grace we tucked in to a good dinner, and enjoyed Annette's cooking. After Patrick's grace, Annette and Patrick discussed matters of dogma, while Alf and I played chess. It continued like this for more than a year. Then, one morning, Alf came into my bedroom. "Annie has run off with Patrick."

I was incredulous; it seemed impossible; and he a man of the cloth; what about their religion, that they were always discussing? And all that about adultery. Did they talk in a code, perhaps, or meet in church? And yes, he was immediately defrocked. That made me wonder about Annette. All too literal; and of course they lost most of their friends. I was the only one who might have been a go-between, but I was never asked. Well, I suppose that's life for you. Alf showed me the note he had found on the kitchen table. It did not say much; just "I'm going, sorry Annette. Alf must sell or give away the clothes I left. Alf was desolate. He asked me to stay with him. We had to say goodbye after my Finals; with promises to keep in touch. We did so, but not for long. We went our separate ways.

One day I bumped into him. He had given up his job as lecturer; the University had tried everything they could to keep him. Alf wanted a new life. But he was glad to see me. It was in another town. We had dinner that night, and chose fish to go with the Pouilly Fuisse. I chatted, on much the same lines as before, but more briefly; Alf had other interests; he was now Head Librarian in a new History Foundation, and had other things to think about. The banks, I told him, had turned crooked again. "What's new?"

That was the main change since we had parted. He told me he had come across Annette, one day. She looked forlorn; she told Alf she was sorry, and she looked it; Patrick had left her for another woman. Annette is now an atheist. She moved to London, and lives now in a rundown quarter of the East End. Alf lives alone. He has had had a string of mistresses, and that is all he needs. The one I met the next night over dinner was a rough sort of girl; she would do for a romp in bed, but as a one-night stand.

I had been married a few years. I knew what could happen if you messed about.

DREAMING

My Lord

It was most kind of you to write with your gracious offer of help. I wonder if I could trouble you to remind me what the matter was on which I was seeking your assistance.

Cheers!

Percival Maltravers

Dear – I presume you are a Mr – Maltravers, I don't know what on earth you are talking about. I have never heard of you. I have sent you no such letter.

Cheers to you!

Pinkwinkle ABC KLM, etc.

My Lord

In the circumstances it was kind of you to reply. I remember now how it was that I came to approach you. I had, the previous night, dreamt that you had written to me. When I woke I was convinced of the truth of this and was so overcome by the great honour you had done me that I sat down at once to write my letter. I see now that it was all an illusion. Please accept my apologies for troubling you.

By the way, how is your cat? I was very upset to hear of her accident.

Cheers!

Percival, etc

Dear Maltravers

My cat is fine. What on earth do you mean by 'accident'? And how did you come to dream about me in the first place? Was it my recent speech in the Lords advocating castration for queers? Was it the interview I gave to the BBC on branding the foreheads of criminals? Or was it that flattering portrait I had commissioned from Charlie Buncle, the one Private Eye got hold of? By the way, I am taking them to court for lack of respect. Strictly between you and me, I rather like the publicity.

Cheery ho!

Pinkwinkle, etc

My Lord

I feel for you a boundless admiration and wish you well in all your fine endeavours.

Cheers as ever!

Percival

I say, Percival, old man. You strike me as a real Englishman. Why don't you hop on a train some time and come up to see me for a spot of lunch. Come to me next Tuesday at the above address

Bottie P. etc

My Lord

I don't understand. On receiving your letter I took the second next train to London – having just missed the first one. From

Waterloo I came hot foot by taxi to your Lordship's house where I asked for your Lordship's secretary to announce my presence. This young lady, wearing a very tight T-shirt and extremely tight jeans, said that your Lordship had said, "Maltravers? Who the hell is he? Chap must be dreaming."

Cheers hopefully!

Percival

Dear Mr Maltravers

My secretary is an impeccably dressed, middle-aged man and an outstanding example of a good clean Englishman. And you, sir, are a dirty old man.

Cheers for once and all!

Pinkwinkle, ABC KLM, etc.

Dear Mr Maltravers

I am Lord Pinkwinkle's secretary, the young lady whom you so graciously mentioned in your letter to his lordship. Bottie is a naughty boy; he should never have asked me to tell you such a porker. If you can suggest any way that I might be of service to you, please let me know.

Yours in anticipation

Plum Pantical

P.S. I have other items of clothing in which you might be interested.

Peter Matthews has a First Class season ticket for his work in London. He enjoys the discreet comfort and the quiet of his single seat. First he reads the main news in the Times, then he puts down the paper to look through the window. He thinks of his responsibilities in serving Lord Porter – Brian to his friends – at his Knightsbridge home. Unlike members of the Lower House, peers are given no facilities for a private assistant. Porter, seeing a need for one, employs Peter as a personal assistant, and provides an office adjoining his own study. Peter is there to research the issues of the day, draft speeches, keep Brian's diary and generally make himself useful in the daily business of an official life.

That morning, Porter tapped the linking door and entered.

"Morning, Peter!"

"Good morning, Brian".

"That draft you gave me yesterday for my speech on the new Justice Bill, it's more or less okay but I'd like a stronger emphasis on how our approach differs from the Government's. They've been veering to the right for some time. They're getting too old-Toryish. Work that in, would you? And let me have something by end of play."

"Sure thing, Brian."

That afternoon, with a good lunch inside him, Peter was returning to work when he saw her coming towards him. He had no idea who she was. He had seen her twice before. Fantasies of her were keeping him from sleep and running riot in his dreams. Her teasing presence had been there as he woke that morning. Here she was now, dressed in T-shirt and tight jeans, the whole curvaceous, lust-inspiring desire for her making him groan inside and avert his eyes in passing her.

There was a wayward demon in his character; he was all too aware of it. How much longer could he conceal it? He had done something stupid in his last job and been lucky to get out with a good reference. And now? There was wilful mischief in the nonsensical letters he posted, correctly addressed to his real self in London to await his arrival. What if illness kept him at home and Brian read them? He wrote the reply from Bottie Pinkwinckle, as he ate his lunch. It shamed him and thrilled him. He put it in the letterbox on his way to Waterloo that evening. The morning post came early. He liked to hear a letter fall on the mat, and liked to read it at as he ate his egg.

He watched the sinking sun on his journey home. A pale-rosy light cast its spell of peace on the fields, hedges and trees. All looked well with the world. He had a wonderful job. He and Porter liked each other. There was one thing, just one thing, that he really must do. He must be a man; conquer timidity; approach her directly and ask her to meet him for lunch. That would be a start. Lust must be consummated without further delay. He must cease forever his feeding frenzy for fantasy. To be done in the manner of a gentleman, of course.

That night he dreamed of a time and a faraway place where angels were girls in T-shirts and tight jeans, clutching him close as they danced on the lawns of Paradise.

MESSAGE TO LYDIA DAVIS

Dear Lydia

I have sent you a short story. If I had more time it would have been shorter.

Love,

Winston.

DISCOVERING

I HAVE BECOME quite fond of my two aunts, Alice and Eloise. They are aunts by mutual adoption, as it were, and throughout my boyhood I called them auntie. I was orphaned at an early age. My parents had no surviving family, and I was formally adopted by a kindly couple who gave me my name, Guy Barnet. I called them Mum and Dad. I see now that with all their good intentions, they turned out to have little sense of what a boy needs. I think they must have been disappointed in me, and perhaps in themselves. I could not give them the love they obviously wanted. It was not in me.

I was twenty years old when I buried them last year. My feelings were sadness rather than grief. And that is sad in itself. My legacy was a small sum and a memory of too much loneliness. Looking back at my boyhood is like watching a film in black and white. The colour was elsewhere. My mum and my dad had all the right instincts, all the right feelings – but in modest amounts. My benefit from that was in not being too fussed over. I was given more independence than the other children I knew. It's not that I was unhappy at home, but I looked elsewhere for engagement in life. I found this in Alice's home.

Alice came on the scene when she found I was in the same class at school as her son George. She saw us as friends. I never really took to George but I quite liked his company, and I was glad to have a friend. We were eight and we got on well enough, for a while. He or his mother would sometimes invite me to spend part of a weekend at their home, just a few streets away. My mum and dad were happy about this. George came sometimes to my place, but we would usually finish at his.

Alice was a kind woman; she gave me a sense of warmth and homeliness. I learnt later that she saw me as a good influence on her difficult son, much as I came to find him a difficult friend. He made me an accomplice in escapades that even I could see were wrong and unkind. I was an unlikely friend for such a boy, and I came to see that my value to him was to point the contrast between the strong and the weak, much as a girl may choose a plain one as companion.

Eloise became my second aunt; I met her often on her visits to her sister. She was unmarried and lived alone. She told me once how much she liked getting away to be with Alice and me. I wondered if she too led a solitary life.

In the summer that I turned ten, Alice asked my Mum if I could come on a two weeks' holiday at their family house in France. Mum and Dad had Bournemouth in mind, but they saw what I preferred. It was an adventure from the start. Alice was sitting in the front, doing the map reading for Mr Ramsay. Aunt Eloise was on the back seat, behind Mr Ramsay; she spoke what must have been good French, and George was next to me.

Their house on the coast had a history for the two sisters. Their father had bought it. When their second daughter was conceived during a holiday there she was given her mother's name in French. And what a lovely place it was: that long, sandy beach and the wide Atlantic beyond. It was Alice's company that

I most valued in those two weeks. George was becoming more difficult. He was aggressive to me and more rebellious to his mother. He got on well with his father; they seemed much of a type. I found them awkward, daunting.

Back home, I saw things changing in that family. Eloise was there more often. Alice was facing the failure of her marriage and needed her sister's support. Underneath his superficial charm and good humour, Mr Ramsey was and always had been a bully. He was selfish; he was indifferent to Alice's wishes and scornful of her opinions. He was quite a lot older than Aunt Alice. She, when they married, was just eighteen. He had enjoyed being loved by such a young, pretty girl. She soon became pregnant and they married. It worked well enough at first, but Alice had to pretend she was happy, now she could do so no longer.

I saw again how like the father the son was. George was a bully and had the same intimidating build and demeanour.

I was eleven years old when I had to move with my parents a whole day's distance away, further north. My dad had found a better job. And that was the time that Alice's divorce came through. She was tearful when I went to say goodbye. She hugged me tight and made me promise to write often. She could keep the house, but wherever she was I must come and stay as often as I liked.

It was difficult to do so. She had taken a job, more to give her something to do and to meet people than because she needed the money. She had won a fair settlement in the divorce court. I managed a few weekend visits during school holidays, but I was growing up and it came to be less pulling. I was upset for her when she wrote of George being expelled from the public school that his father had sent him to. She told me later that he had slept with the headmaster's daughter and stolen some of her jewellery. Almost funny, except to the ones who suffered.

I think for both of us the relationship found a lower emotional level. She told me to call her Alice; I did so while still thinking of her as an honorary aunt. She gave me news of Eloise, but some years would pass before I saw either of them again. She gave me news of George. He had scorned university and found a well paid job in the City. Alice hinted at an irregular private life. I could see she was still a worried mother. I wrote to tell her of my successes at school and university, the First that I won and then the PhD. She sent me a card with a cheque on every birthday and we always exchanged Christmas cards. Hers came with another cheque – until my twenty-first birthday. What more could one ask from an aunt?

Time passed. I am now in my late thirties. I've not done too badly, considering how I started. My boyhood days are well behind me and well forgotten. If chance should evoke the past, it comes, still, in black and white; but there is more colour in the life now. I remember once hearing a clinical word for my so-called 'condition'. I looked it up in the dictionary, shrugged it off and did not believe it anyway. I do now feel more connected with life. I have a girl friend, Julie. We live separately but we get along quite well and there are things we do together. She has a nice little house. I have a flat overlooking the campus of my university.

I have been in the same department of Philosophy at the University where I took my two Degrees. I see little reason to move elsewhere, and even less now that I have the Chair. I hold on to the good things in my life; they give it continuity. Alice and Eloise are part of it; we had never totally lost touch. They have retired from life in England and live now in France, in the house where I had stayed with them one wonderful holiday as a ten-year old.

It has become a habit for me to rent somewhere in France for my long summer vacations. I wanted a small town with a river flowing through it, and I finally found what I wanted it in the region around Poitiers. I liked the profound silence I could always find in the surrounding country, and town and coast were not far away. I went every year, and sometimes twice. I took work; I had the peace to prepare lectures or get an article finished. When I got my Chair I bought the house I had seen and longed for in just such a small town with a river flowing through it. I renamed my house Découverte. I had discovered it, much as I was now discovering myself. I love it there the more I go. It was a happy choice for another reason. The house of my aunts was on that coast that was not far distant from my new home. Going there, and perhaps on my return, I make the short detour to spend two or three nights with them. Their kindness is as it ever was. In return, I tell myself, I am keeping an eye on them. I make a point of asking what I can do or buy for them in England. They are, I guess, in their mid fifties now, and continue to display the fondness of aunts. I confess I enjoy their admiration for my academic success and their questions on what I have published. They laughingly disclaim any understanding of it.

Alice has kept her looks, if not enhanced them, and Eloise is as feminine as ever. What I notice now of Eloise is her vulnerability. I see her as an easy target for the sort of man who would seduce her, and flee on the midnight hour, leaving others to clear up the mess. Unless, perhaps, he were to stay for the money. There must have been a good inheritance from their father. Alice also had the money from her divorce settlement. Of course, I had no idea what she was worth.

I have never taken Julie on these trips. Her holidays are more limited than mine, and the timing is awkward for her. She has flown down once or twice, but we have to admit that France does not thrill her very much. I have mentioned her to Alice, who tells me I must bring her, but it has never worked out.

They live well together, the sisters. Alice, the older and more practical, is the manager. She takes the decisions. Eloise is unworldly. She is still the spinster and accepts the term, signing herself as Miss. She is feminine and unaffected by feminism. She is aware, though, of what it now means to be a bachelor girl, and sometimes jokes of it. All this has little resonance among the small community of English in the closed settlement they have made for themselves. They strike me, the ones I have met, as people with limited interests and vocabulary.

Alice and Eloise have settled down there, with their little rituals for passing the day. They come to life each morning for their 'elevenses'. It is more of an event if taken in a café with others. Luncheon, as they like to call it, is a high point. After that a gap yawns until the coming of tea and cakes renews the daily rhythm that builds to a peak at the evening meal. It is not that they are obsessed by food and drink, but it does provide a focus for their comment. They think of the next meal as does a patient in hospital. It is the next event. Naturally it is a standard topic, along with the weather, in the company of their English friends.

They have found all the places that serve food and drink in the settlement and the villages around. There are endless comparisons for their discussion.

"Jean-Claude does serve a good cup of coffee", one will say.

"Pierre's coffee is not quite as good, I agree", another adds, "but he seems to know the sort of biscuits that we English like".

And at the taking of afternoon tea in one of these cafes you might hear, "Of course, coming to France we can't really expect the locals to do it as we are used to. It reminds you that you're in a foreign country, don't you think?"

"Gladys was telling me just the other day that Michel serves the most delicious cakes you can imagine."

"Oh, but we must go then."

With the coming of Spring, evenings take on a special quality for the two women. They can sit outdoors on the patio, in the little garden that overlooks the sea. On the first warm evening they will take their aperitif outside before going in for dinner; soon they will be dining outside, and in high summer they go all the way through to the last digestif imprinting its flavour on the pleasure of gazing upon the wide extravagances of sea and sky stretched out before them. These are the poetic moments that justify their chosen exile. I too feel the joy and grandeur of it. But I see too the limited range of their pleasures and the seeming banalities of their social life. I think that Alice may be less enamoured of it than Eloise. I wonder about them.

From time to time, on my visits, Alice tells me of her concern for son George. His work in the City has made him extremely rich, but given him a reputation for sailing close to the wind. As Alice understands it, George's natural ability at mathematics enables him to create financial products of such complexity that only he will know how to sell them. And he is not bothered when some of his clients are left with large losses. It's their fault, not his. The financial press, in which he has previously been admired, now refers to him as aggressive, ruthless and unethical. Scandals are widely reported, but he courts publicity regardless. He will boast of spending tens of thousands of pounds on wine at bonus-celebrating dinners. Alice is not a prude, but this blatantly degenerate life disturbs her. Even worse are the stories of his marriages and infidelities.

Worst of all for Alice is George's attitude to her, his mother. It is usually she who must ring him, and never in these exchanges does he show signs of pleasure or affection, let alone love. He talks dismissively of his working life. When she speaks of something she has read in her English paper, he tells her not to believe all that rubbish. His life and his wife fare fine, just fine, you know? much as ever. And George always asks her the standard questions, how are things at your end? good weather? Eloise OK? Alice might try to chat, but there is little in return. It is the same when it is he who rings her. When George puts the phone down with a goodbye Mum, before she has finished, Alice is angry. She despairs of him.

"How did he get like this, Guy? Where did we fail, as parents? Where did I fail as a mother? I'm not a prig, as you know, but surely you have to draw the line somewhere. He seems to lack, totally lack, any moral sense."

"It's a perennial problem, Alice; I see it happening to many of my students' parents; you're not alone. I might say, it's a problem I shall avoid by not having children." I leant forward. "You must not blame yourself. George had a good family life. Then he grew up. He made friends. Experimented. He discovered what he liked, and the sort of people he wanted around him. The City's a tough life and it does things to you. Well that's how I see it. Now, look at what you have here. You have a wonderful life with Eloise and your friends. Relax. Let me pour you another glass". I knew this was inadequate. I was evading her problem, but it was all I could do on the spur of the moment. But she was often in my thoughts and I wished I could help.

George is a continuing worry for his mother. Occasionally she manages to see him for a night or two in London. He has to find time to fit her in, time perhaps for a late dinner at a local restaurant.; but they don't find much to say to each other. He brings a wife or mistress; she too would be working in the City. George has twice been to France to see his mother and each time came accompanied by a different, unexplained woman. It is no life for a mother.

On one of my visits, sitting outside with Alice while Eloise took her turn to wash up after dinner, she said in a sad tone, how she regretted George had not turned out more like me. The return of Eloise made a reply unnecessary.

I got to my house the following day and couldn't help noticing the many improvements it needed to make it more comfortable. This would raise its value and I could sell it for something better. I had my eye on a special house, just outside of the town, with the lovely river flowing peacefully past. I yearned for it.

You must never think that I had a mercenary motive for visiting Alice. It must have been George at the back of my mind that prompted thoughts of money.

Departmental duties and staff problems kept me in England during the Easter break. It was not till the following summer that I could call on my aunts. I found a newcomer there, Oswald. He made a fourth in the core group of Alice and Eloise and their closes friend, Gladys. Gladys was a big-bosomed, blowsy woman. Starting as barmaid in a pub, she was now the successful owner and manager of her own bar and restaurant. She loved cooking almost as much as she loved eating. She was great fun to be with, a woman with the common touch and an uninhibited humour that verged on the coarse. She was quite unlike Alice and Eloise, and that made me see them in a new light. They were not as old-fashioned as they sometimes appear, I was glad to think.

I arrived, as usual, on a Saturday, knowing that the peak event of their week was the Saturday dinner at the better of the two most favoured restaurants. It was there that I met Oswald. He had appeared in the settlement just five weeks before and was already one of them – the only man among the three women. He looked a few years younger than them, but not enough to make a difference. There was an easy-going acceptance about him. He warmed to the same topics of conversation, with nuggets of memory to offer from a wider experience of life. They sat at the same table every Saturday; and that night it had been set with five places.

"It's interesting the way that no one talks these days about spinsters", Oswald said, extending the drift of a conversation, "in fact, it seems to be incorrect these days to use the word." He looked at Eloise. "And you, Eloise, are a bachelor girl, are you not? The world is your oyster."

I could not swear to it, but I think she blushed. I had not seen it before. She looked unsure how to respond; she had no joke ready.

"You're partial to oysters, aren't you, dear?" said Gladys, enjoying the moment.

Alice added, "Oswald brings a freshness to our conversation, Guy; he livens us up."

The waiter, coming with our main course, brought with it the next topic, started by Eloise with an air of relief at being able to do so.

Oswald invited us round for drinks the next morning, after Mass. He was the only one of the group who attended Sunday service. In the short time he had lived here he had made his mark on the traditional, rather dull French cottage interior, where he lived. The cottage was small; daily life was all on the ground floor, with an attic used only for storage. It was freshly painted and simply but well furnished. In a glimpse through the briefly opened bedroom door I saw bare white walls and a cross above his bed, but his well-stocked drinks cabinet reminded me of what it means to have a catholic taste. He was in an expansive mood, talking of the women he had noticed in church. He said the young pretty ones more than compensated for the older countrywomen who adopted widowhood black before their time. I had the impression he was aiming his conversation at Eloise, while she had an air of alertness that was new to her.

I left on the Monday morning. Alice came out to the car with me.

"Things seem to be getting worse with George," she said in a bleak voice. "He's asked if he can spend a week here, perhaps longer, some time in August. I suppose you couldn't drop in here, on your way back? Not that you'd like to see him, but it might be a comfort for me, to talk things over with you. Can I give you a ring?"

I reflected, as I drove to my house, how my relationship with Alice had changed in recent years. She was no longer an aunt, she was a friend, much as I was her's, and no longer a nephew. Had I, in some way, become a proxy son?

The next weeks in my new home were better than ever. Julie, again, was unable to join me, but I found a lot to do and I thought happily of all the things I might do one day. I engaged a young schoolteacher to give me French conversation for an hour every morning. On the last day of August, Alice rang.

"Guy, I'm at my wits' end. Eloise has gone off with Oswald. And George is here, sacked by his bank and possibly facing criminal charges. Please, please come."

I arrived the following evening. George had gone for a walk and Alice lost no time in telling me about his downfall. An all too familiar story. I gave Alice what comfort I could and asked after her sister.

"There was something going on between them. It was obvious from the start. Did you notice?" I nodded. "Perhaps it was mutual; I just don't know. Eloise was obviously deeply struck. She has fallen in love for the first time in her life. At her age! She's been too protected all these years. The trouble is, Guy, I'm not sure about him. He seems a man of the world, in so far as a schoolmaster can be. He never let the conversation go very far on the subject."

She paused. "There's been a lot in the press lately about

schoolmasters." She took my hand. "I'm worried sick, Guy."

George came through the door from the garden. Alice stood back and said, "George, here's Guy." She looked at the two of us. "Do you recognise each other."

"Hi, I'd know you anywhere. Still the same serious look. How're you doing?" he said, grinning and offering a weak handshake. Alice went into the kitchen to prepare the meal. George and I went out to the garden. He put a glass and a bottle of wine on the table for me, and a glass and bottle of whisky for himself. He had a large one.

"I'm in deep shit. I expect Alice has told you."

"In general terms. I know too little about your work and your world to say much about it."

"Well, don't bother then. Tell me about yourself. You do something brainy, I think Alice said."

I was happy to keep away from his problems. I did not want to listen to him. I spoke of my academic life, my personal life, my love of France and my French home. I spoke slowly to spin it out. I did not mind boring him, as I obviously did. I kept it going till Alice brought out the food. She and I chatted about local affairs, about the people we knew, and about life in France. George said little and drank whisky throughout the meal. Half way through dessert he stood up and said he needed a walk. Alice went through to the kitchen. I followed her a moment later. She was standing over the sink, sobbing her heart out. I pulled her into my arms. "Alice, poor dear Alice, it'll be all right," I said, patting her back. She clung to me, till I gently pulled away from her.

We were silent, clearing away the remains of the meal and tidying up in the kitchen. She said to go to bed; she would sit there waiting for George. At her suggestion, I left the next morning. She said thank you when we kissed goodbye. I did not see George.

Oswald was convicted of paedophilia and sent to prison. Eloise was convinced of his genuine remorse and his pledge to reform. She would stand by him. She would help him and lead him to a new life. He was loving and grateful. She bought a small flat close to the prison so she could visit him as often as allowed. Such a strange, imperfect way to find fulfilment, and so late in life. But what strange ways love can take. One had to admire her and hope her faith would be justified. She kept in close touch with Alice, who came to accept the new arrangement, though she had grave doubts as to Oswald's motive. Was it genuine affection, or just cover? The sisters were now committed to living apart. Alice would never again want to live in England. Eloise could never again face the English in that tight, gossipy community. Poor Eloise. Oswald deserted her, reoffended and was returned to prison. Eloise died of a broken heart.

George too went to prison. The details of his case were sordid and I make no further comment. Alice, steeling herself with a sense of duty, wrote to him regularly. His replies were brief, infrequent and unsettling. What could she do, with a son like that?

I had sometimes wondered how committed Alice was to her home and way of life in that artificial community. She had hinted more than once that Eloise had the stronger attachment. And so, on my visit the following spring, I collected Alice and drove her to my French home. She loved it there and welcomed my suggestion that I bring her down for a longer stay in the summer. I did that. In the evening of our first day we were standing by the open door to the garden. There was a soft orange light on the river and all was well with the world outside. I turned to her and we stood for a moment in silence. She was still. I started to speak.

"Alice, it's strange. I have been discovering so much about myself. There has been something coming to the surface for I don't know how long but is now right in front me and overwhelms me. It is you. Alice, my Alice, I have fallen in love with you. Please be kind to me."

In that unforgettable moment her eyes widened, her lips opened and she was in my arms. We kissed and clung till she felt me grow against her and she led me to bed. We had a late dinner and got drunk on champagne and I was as happy as I had ever been.

She told me she would buy us a bigger house and furnish it for the two of us. "For my dotage," she said, "and your retirement … and make that an early one."

Back at my university I gave a year's notice. I saw Julie and told her what had happened. I felt sorry for her, not for losing me but for my never giving her the attention and affection that she might have expected.

Alice aged well. We were happy in our new life in the house I had yearned for and Alice had bought. We made friends, explored France and travelled abroad. Everything we did had its mutual comfort. It was enough just being together. And we grew older together. It must be true, I told her, about the eye of the beholder. So, at the last, I had made my discoveries. I had discovered life and love. I had discovered my self. I told her often of my love for her and she told me she loved me as the son she had once wished for and she loved me as the husband she had once wished for but she loved me above all for who I am and that for me was the greatest love of all. We had our moments of high passion; they made their point in the calm years that remained to us. Came the day I must bury her in this place; I wept and wept. I had discovered grief.

LYDIA DAVIS WAS SPEECHLESS

THE CYCLIST

MARK ADAMS is cycling to collect his morning paper. He has the look of a young man without a care in the world. It is a fresh, sunny spring day; he loves to see the fresh tulips in the gardens that he passes on this quiet, residential street. He loves to feel his long blond hair ruffling gently behind him, the hair that girls tell him they envy.

It is an easy pedal up the gentle slope of this road. He loves and cherishes his green Dawes touring cycle; he is proud of its 5-3-1 alloy construction, and he cleans it daily. He pedals and thinks of Anna, his new girl friend. He has not met her type before. She is clever in ways that he is not. He tells his friends that she graduated last year from Cambridge, with a First in European Literature. "Out of your class, mate", a friend told him. "Rubbish, I've got skills she hasn't", he replied. What's more, she's fantastic in bed." It's the attraction of opposites, he said.

His daydreams ended with a bang as he smashed his head against the back of a parked car. He heard the loud clash of metal, he felt the thud of his head as it hit the rear window; and then the flash of lights that he would say was "like seeing stars for the first time ever". Coming to, he was aware of a wet trickle down the side of his face. His neck and shoulders hurt and he could not move. He had a throbbing head. Coming to for the second time he heard the sound of rapid footsteps. His wrist was lifted and a finger placed on his pulse. He opened his eyes. Only an angel from heaven could have such a lovely face, and so beautifully framed with auburn hair. She knelt close and he felt an irresistible urge to kiss her, but could not move.

"Don't try to move, just tell me where it hurts." She put his wrist down. "Your pulse seems all right. Now, where's the most pain?" She had taken out her mobile.

He gave her a small smile, already thinking how best to play the scene.

"I hurt all over, but I don't think anything's broken."

She dialled 999 and called for an ambulance. She was squatting now, beside him.

"This is why people wear a helmet when they cycle. If they're half sensible."

"Yes, ma'am", he says with a weak smile.

"Are you always so irresponsible?"

"Yes, ma'am." He is able to laugh. "You're making me feel better already. Tell me, is my cycle badly damaged?"

She picked it up. "The handles are a bit skew, but it's movable. But you've left your marks on the car," she said, inspecting it. "The paint is scratched, and there's a dent, see, here? You'll have to let the police know. Perhaps the ambulance crew will do that."

"Yes, but my bike?" he said, a pleading look in his eyes.

"What about your bike?"

He lay there with a helpless look, waiting.

She asked, with a hint of vexation, "Do you live near?"

He gave the address of the small house he had just come from.

"Well, that's quite near, I suppose. If I push it round for you, is there somewhere I can leave it?"

"You are a true angel of mercy. You could wheel it down the

alley on the left side of the house, if you really don't mind, and leave it up against the back wall. I shall be home soon enough." He gave her the address.

The ambulance arrived, the blare of its klaxon winding down as it pulled up behind them. The two paramedics quickly confirmed that no bones were broken. He might be mildly concussed; and his head wound will need stitching. They will take him to the local A&E. "Just lie there while we get the stretcher."

Mark looks at the young woman, now backing away with his cycle.

"I don't know your name."

She hesitated. "Susan."

"I'm Mark. Will you do me one last favour?"

"What?"

"Come and see me in hospital."

She stares at him.

"Why should I do that?"

"Please!"

"You're a spoilt boy. I may look in this afternoon, if I have time."

She sets off before he can answer, and he is carried off on the stretcher.

"You're a lucky bloke by the look of it."

In the ambulance, he remembers Anna. Well, he'll have to sort it out – but not just yet. He is a realist; he knows from experience that the flames of desire fade all too easily when a new one comes along. One girl leads to another. The knack was to keep them blissfully ignorant for as long as possible, while gradually withdrawing.

The ambulance arrived. He was carried in and they classified him as accident but not emergency. He was left on a trolley. After a while a nurse checked his wound and told him he must lie till the doctor saw him. Any time after six o'clock.

He fell asleep and woke up in a bed. And there was the angelic face looking down at him as he woke. Heaven indeed.

"I dropped in to tell you that I've put your bike where you asked me to."

She had pushed her chair back to look at him, and to be out of hands' reach.

"You're very kind. What would make me now leap out of bed is to hear you say that you came because you wanted to see me again."

It took off from there. She accepted the challenge of flirting. He summoned his utmost charm and found ever more daring innuendo. She played along while keeping her distance. There was a hint of primness that he found erotic.

He thought of Anna: intellectual, less pretty but physically passionate. In Susan he sensed virginity – could it be? And with that thought came a vision of the future, the special blessing that may fall upon the young as manna from heaven. Life is before you. Everything is still possible.

Susan looked at her watch.

"I must go, Mark. I've loved our little talk; and I shall never forget you. The cyclist who recycles his girl friends! You're marvellous! Anna didn't tell you she has a sister, did she? Oh, the promises you made! We couldn't stop laughing."

SOFTWARE

I LIVE ON the outer reaches of the Universe. The planet Copernicus and I are the sole remaining survivors from Big Bang. The next one was called Little Bang. I have had my eye on planet Earth for some time. It is made of different stuff. It might be safe for me. When Copernicus had succumbed to the predicted onslaught of spam, it will be no more than the flash of a second; and coding will mingle with the other mist of coding around it. All will be lost in the dust of creation. jj%6ch<>;? is an example. I shall be the only carrier of hardware in the Universe. What can I do?

I took the plunge; I trusted my luck to the environment on Earth. It surprised and amazed me. Earthlings live wonderful lives. I landed among them on a small island called Sardinia and was soon put on a ship to England. When I arrived I found the most wonderful things. I saw landscape; I heard music, and I went travelling. I learnt English in a flash, and a lot of other languages at the same time. The most wonderful thing of all was the opposite sex. I had been programmed as a male and now I was meeting the most beautiful women. The loveliest of all was Gudrun. She was German, and lived in England. I taught her all the European languages and helped her with Mandarin Chinese. Whether it was that or my funny appearance, we fell in love and married. We make a good team.

Oh, and Copernicus disappeared, as expected.

THE MYSTERIOUS
MRS WILMINGTON

"I JUST LOVE the Slavic face", Mike said, "there's something about it, something in the structure, the high, slanting cheekbones. You may remember, some years ago I had that holiday in Prague. A lovely city, but one thing I specially remember is the haunting quality of some of the faces I saw. Men as well as women, equally beautiful, but it's seeing that face in women that really gets me."

It was a Saturday morning about two years ago, and Mike and I were having lunch together in our favourite pub. We were old friends. It had become a custom to meet like this, to talk, review our weeks, chat at random and enjoy the beer and some good nosh.

Mike was, and still is, working in London with an accounting firm. I also, at that time, commuted, though usually on a later train. The train service at the time I speak of had been suspended for two weeks, after a minor collapse in a tunnel. I could work at home if I had to but Mike had to get to his office. That meant using the temporary bus service. It was on the second morning, queuing for the bus, that Mike saw her.

But I must let Mike tell the story in his own words, as well as I remember them. I give them here, edited to make it more readable. Then I'll tell my story.

"She was behind me in the queue that Tuesday morning, though at some distance, and all I could see of her face was a line of cheek framed with hair. She wore a light topcoat, suitable for April, but that April morning was wintry and she must have been cold. The coat was an old one and far from fashionable. The squared pattern of green and oatmeal would have been smart once, I imagine. It went well with her hair. Her hair had that shade of red that's nearly autumnal. It was blowing loosely in the wind and I was strangely moved, looking at her.

"You'll remember, the tunnel had collapsed at the weekend and train services were suspended on the first day of April. That was a Monday. Which is why I know that it was Tuesday the second of April two years ago that I had my first sight of her.

"We were queuing for the bus they'd laid on. What stood out was her stillness. I was stamping impatiently at the cold, flapping my arms and turning against the wind. She did not move. The hang of her coat suggested a slim, straight figure, with the wind at times picking out the shape beneath. Her stillness suggested an inner absorption. It gave her the quality of sculpture. I waited for her to turn to give me a full view of her face, which she did when the bus came; but she looked straight past me. I was looking straight at her and she hadn't noticed me. I got on the bus before her, hoping to get a close look at this strange, and yes, beautiful woman. Were those green eyes troubled, I wondered, or had she just had a bad night? They were haunting eyes.

"I know what you're thinking. I have romantic fancies.

"When she came to board, the bus was full and the conductor put out an arm to bar her. It was three days, the Friday, before I saw her again. I had been wanting to see her again. I dreamed of her before going to sleep at night. Justin, you're not the only person who's told me I should focus on the practical business of choosing a wife. Well, perhaps this was it. I was aware of time passing and this woman had certainly cast her spell. She no longer had the bloom of youth; she must have been a few years older than me, probably mid to late thirties. But so what? I had seen a wedding ring. Was she unhappily married? Was her husband unfaithful? Cruel? I would be as a source of comfort, I thought.

"The next time in the queue was different. She was standing right in front of me. She turned to look across the road. I stood still, looking down, not wanting her to see me staring. It's hard to describe this, but I remembered a football match I played at school in my last year. I was centre forward. In those last few moments, with the tension and noise rising from the sidelines, for us on the field the volume fell away. We played in a cone of silence. And that's how I felt that morning. Well, the bus came and she went inside. I had to sit upstairs.

"That Saturday, walking down the High Street for my weekly shopping, I saw her talking to the man, Gregory Jones, the Welshman, you know? I quickened my pace hoping he could introduce me, but by the time I reached him she had slipped inside a hairdresser's shop. I stood chatting to Gregory, finally mentioning that I thought I knew that woman he'd just been talking to. I said I'd seen her a few times at the bus stop.

"'Oh of course, you're on the bus while they sort out the tunnel' he said. The subject of trains and buses occupied us for a few minutes, and then, 'Yes, that's Mrs Wilmington. I don't really know her but her husband was a friend of my brother-in-law. Wilmington is quite a bit older than his wife. I met him once. Funny sort of chap. I heard he kept her short of money.

Can't say I took to him. But no accounting for tastes. Though I do sometimes wonder how much choice there was in the matter. Mind you, that was some time ago. Don't know what's happened since. And no chance to ask her just now – great hurry to say hello and goodbye and she must get her hair done. But all may not be as well as it should be. Still, mustn't speculate. Good Lord, must dash. Bye'. And he was gone, in typical Gregory fashion, leaving a cluster of abbreviated sentences scattered behind him.

"This all too brief account of Mr Wilmington's wife gave extra fuel to my thoughts. No husband worthy of such a woman could fail to worship her. Perhaps she was now a grieving widow. Or, better, divorced. There were too many questions and I thought of all the good answers.

"On the Friday morning of the second week I stood in the queue for the third and last time. Train services resumed on the Monday. She's behind me in the queue. The bus comes and I step onto it. She hesitates. It pulls away and she runs forward. She looks me full in the face, smiling. It must be the first time she's noticed me. I try to grab her hand but the bus speeds away.

"I did not see Mrs Wilmington again. I'd seen her just those three times. The memory faded. And then I met Jennifer. Six months later we married, and your speech as best man was terrific. Well, you've seen the two of us together often enough. She's the perfect wife. We're a practical couple, we laugh a lot and we love each other. In the early days I would sometimes remember how I once yearned for someone else; and how lucky I now was to have got over it. I can't imagine wanting anyone else as my wife. Nor could I want a mistress."

I'm glad Mike found his true happiness. Jennifer is just right for him. On Saturdays there are now four of us who meet for lunch. I've found my happiness too. Mary enchants me. We married after her divorce came through. I must never tell her how Mike had once yearned for her; it would betray him, and cause embarrassment to them both. We make a very good foursome. Before I introduced her to the other couple, I said to her, "I wonder if you noticed Mike in the bus queue, the time the tunnel was blocked." No, she didn't remember anyone in the queue; all she could remember of that time was how miserable she was about her marriage. When they met, that first time, Mary said, "Justin tells me we stood in the same bus queue two years ago, when the tunnel was blocked." Jennifer lifted an eyebrow, they all laughed, and that was that.

Mike and I still meet for a pint or two, and have our little chat. Wednesday evenings suit us best. We joked once or twice about my marrying his mysterious Mrs Wilmington. I told him I was sorry not having him as best man at my wedding, but on her second time round Mary wanted a quiet one in a registry office.

Dear Mike, once the romantic, impractical dreamer, and now such a sound, sensible fellow. But I do sometimes wonder. Is that a wistful look I see in his eye? And I see Jennifer, the way she looks at him.

Mary, I should explain, was born in England to English parents, but her grandmother was Czech. And yes, that Slavic face enchants me. I know I got the better deal.

CIRCLES

BERTHILDE, or Bertie, as she liked to be called, had been sleeping badly. She was almost sure that she loved Tom, and almost sure that Tom loved her – but with less ardour. Tom was an easygoing young man and that was one of the things she liked in him. They shared the expectation of a future together; it was the easy thing to do. But sometimes, at night, she sensed another man, a dark man inside her, circling her round and round, his eyes burning and she as his prey.

She and Tom believed in equality between man and woman and they applied the principle to their daily lives; and so, over time, they came to an agreement on the labours and positions of love. He chose them on Monday, Wednesday and Friday. She chose them on Tuesday, Thursday and Saturday. Sunday was a day of rest. This had been their custom now for three years. They marked the date of it in their diaries, as a special anniversary. And on the same day – it was the tenth of May– they discussed and agreed the time and place for their annual holidays.

We have not been to Spain. We should try Barcelona, or travel through Extremadura. This was Tom's idea.

We have not been to Germany. We should try Dresden, or travel through Bavaria. This was Bertie's idea.

They agreed on Paris together in June; and on the agreed week in September, Tom would go to Spain and Bertie would go to Germany.

They enjoyed Paris, in a relaxed sort of way. They liked to sit at a pavement table, eating, drinking and watching people. Tom laughed at all the loving couples. Bertie did not laugh; she was envious. Those couples were enjoying themselves in a way that she and Tom never did; they were happy in their mutual gazing, their touching and kissing. And all done in public.

Tom said, "How lucky we are, you and me, in our sensible way of loving."

Bertie smiled and put her hand on his, then looked away. Tom was not the romantic type. He was sensible. He had the practical virtues. He managed the house and paid the bills on time. He put up shelves and knew what to do in the garden.

But she asked herself, yet again, is there nothing more than this? Where is the romance and the passion?

September came. Tom was in Barcelona and Bertie in Bamberg.

Bertie found a café she liked where she could sit at a pavement table and watch the people. She remembered her thoughts, doing this with Tom, in Paris in June.

On her second morning, waiting to order her coffee, a man approached her table and said, "May I join you? It is busy today."

"Of course."

He had a pleasant voice. He spoke good English but she could see that he was German. He thanked her and smiled as he sat down.

"English, I think?"

"Is it so obvious? Yes, and a tourist."

"Ah!"

They sat looking at each other.

The waiter came and they ordered.

"If you permit, my name is Siegfried. Siegfried Mann, at your service."

"I have never met a Siegfried. My name is Bertie. Bertie Ashton. I was christened with a name from Old English; it is also Old German and you may know it: Berthilde."

He gave a start.

"I do know it. Its meaning in German is woman warrior. My name also is Old German. It means prince of peace. But it is what Wagner made of it in the Ring Cycle that comes strongly to mind".

They were wide-eyed and quiet. A smile came to each of them.

"Wagner took the name Brünnhilde from the Norse sagas. I expect you know the story?"

"Vaguely. I have never seen it".

"You must. Brünnhilde, virtually your namesake, was a Valkyrie, the tribe of great women warriors. Her father, Wotan, left her on a mountaintop surrounded by a circle of fire. It was a punishment for disobedience. Her only hope of rescue would be the coming of a hero, brave and strong enough to extinguish the fire and take her as his own. Siegfried was that hero".

He sat up straight and bowed in the German fashion.

"It is a story. I tell it without presumption".

"The coincidence of our meeting like this is a story in itself. But if you will excuse me, I must pay for my coffee and leave you to yours. I shall call the waiter."

"Please, I insist, the coffee is on me."

He paused and looked at her.

"Perhaps you will give me the pleasure of lunch one day? Tomorrow?"

Why not? She gave a respectable pause. She agreed on tomorrow, at this café, at twelve-thirty.

At their third meeting they were talking again of the Ring Cycle.

"If anyone were to rescue me, it would have to be Tom."

There. She had found the moment to tell him of Tom.

He bowed slightly. A formal man.

"Your husband? Partner?"

"Partner. We've been together now for several years."

"It is common here, too, but I am old-fashioned. When I find a woman to love with true passion it shall be for life as man and wife. I would tell her to imagine herself in a circle of fire, a shield to protect our marriage. It would be a fire to daunt any man rash enough to face my wrath."

Bertie trembled. This was the dark man himself, sitting before her. She looked at him. Neither was smiling. His eye had a deep look. He was every inch a hero.

He said, "Passion may fade, over the years from the front of a lover's mind. It fades but never dies; it is the essential part of one's being and must be the ruling principal of a marriage. Permit me to ask, is this your experience?"

She could not answer.

"Berthilde, you tremble."

His hand reached out to cover hers.

"We, you and I, have come a long way very quickly. I see you with depths of great passion. Be brave. Now. Let me encircle you."

She could but murmur her surrender, "Yes."

Meanwhile Tom had found a café he liked in Barcelona, where he sat outside and watched people. He remembered his thoughts, sitting like this with Bertie in Paris, in June. Something had struck him then, something in her manner and look, at one particular moment. He looked at the couples now in a fresh light, wondering if something lacked in his loving.

"Mind if I join you? It's busy today."

"Please do."

She sounded English. She fussed with things in her handbag and looked cross. She gave Tom a casual glance and called the waiter. She ordered brusquely. She sighed with relief when her coffee came, drank it quickly and sat back.

"I'm bad tempered until I've drunk my first coffee."

She was quite pretty, in a used sort of way. She cocked an eye at him and smiled.

"Are you a tourist?"

He nodded.

"Would you like me to show you some sights?"

She raised an eyebrow and made a suggestive pause.

"Or would you just like some fun?"

Questions rushed through Tom's mind. Could he carry the burden of infidelity? Would the experience show him the strength, or the weakness, of his love for Bertie? Would it be expensive? He took his time, like a reasonable man.

"Okay, may as well. We'll have some fun."

Bertie was home by seven in the evening. Tom walked in half an hour later. They kissed and embraced with the customary signs of affection. Over supper, Tom told Bertie about Barcelona: the cathedral, the sights, the hotel where he stayed and the restaurants and cafes he had visited. He told her almost everything he had done. Bertie then told Tom about her holiday, in similar detail. They went to bed. It was a Sunday and they had a quiet night.

At supper the next evening, they spoke, in a desultory way, of their separate holidays. They sat afterwards, on the sofa, each waiting for the other to speak.

Tom was first.

"Well", he said, "I think I should tell you – please help me, this will be difficult – I have felt for some time that we have not been as close as we should. We noticed it in Paris, didn't we?"

Bertie, wide-eyed, could only nod.

"I was unfaithful to you, one afternoon in Barcelona. And I saw that, ordinary as the experience was, I did not feel as guilty as I should.

"Bertie", and he put his hand on hers, "are you mad at me? Was this a step too far? Oh, my dear you're crying."

"Dear Tom, I'm sad it comes to this after our years together. But you are right. And now I confess. I too was unfaithful, and I did feel guilty. I told him I had you, and that mattered. Now, let us take as long as we need, but perhaps we should think of living apart."

Tom had put up a camp bed for himself in the sitting room, to make it easier for Bertie. He lay awake for some time before sleeping. He had not told Bertie that he had paid for a whore. It would lower him in her estimation – and, anyway, the woman had given little enough pleasure for the money he had to pay. Afterwards it had felt unsavoury. But if the idea was approached in an open and practical way, he thought, why not just pay for sex when you want it? It would give you an endless variety of women and with none of the costs and responsibilities of living with the one woman. I shall get a flat. I shall write a novel, he thought, as he fell asleep.

Bertie, too, lay awake for some time, on her own in the double bed. She did not want to hurt Tom by telling him of the great passion aroused by another man. But she had fallen deeply and irredeemably in love. Just a moment of aberration, she had told him – but there had been two nights and two whole days when she had been so wonderfully ravished by Siegfried, who begged for her hand in marriage.

"After what we have done", Siegfried told her, "there can be no other woman in the world that I could love. Please, please end it with Tom and come back to me soon. My darling Bertie, we shall have our circle of fire, for ever and ever".

"Darling Siegfried, I am yours for ever."

She fell asleep, now, seeing Siegfried above her, kissing her all over.

OH, THE CHILDREN, THE CHILDREN

"OH, what adorable little children!" She spoke with the rapture of a woman without her own. She bent over them, beaming. Angela and Richard smiled back at her. Angela – so often called angelic – and Richard – "such a darling little boy" – were at the front door, shaking hands with their friends, after the party for their sixth birthday. They were twins, and their parents were very proud of them.

Later that evening, tucked up in bed and having been read to by their father, they talked of the party.

"Who was that stupid woman; the one who called us adorable', Angela said, spinning out that last word.

"She's sloppy, that's what I call her", Richard replied. "I'd like to put a drawing pin on her chair to stick into her fat bottom when she sat down".

Angela giggled. "Ooh yes; and she's not the only one. Our teacher's another".

"I dare you", said Richard.

"All right. You'll see".

Next morning, as the class assembled, Richard played his agreed part. He diverted attention by pretending to fall over, letting Angela put a drawing pin on teacher's chair. She had glued its head to make sure it stayed there. Miss Smith, the teacher, came in and said, "Good morning, children!"

"Good morning, teacher!" they replied. Teacher pulled out the chair and sat down. She leapt up at once screaming "ouch!" and clutching her bottom. She looked down at the chair, and was very angry.

"Who did this?"

Silence.

"Who did it?" more loudly. "Own up, or I shall tell the headmistress".

Silence.

She left the classroom and the children all looked at each other. No one looked guilty. The headmistress entered the classroom, and asked them who had done it. No one owned up, and they were all given lines.

The twins had learnt their first lesson. They looked too angelic to be suspected of such a misdeed.

After their ninth birthday party, they lay in bed waiting for their parents to kiss them goodnight.

"Wouldn't you like a room of your own now?" they asked.

"Oh no, thank you! We like to sleep together".

The parents exchanged glances. They'll learn all too soon what that means, their faces said.

"Well all right, darlings, for one more year. And now, don't keep yourselves awake talking too long".

Angela looked happy when the door was shut.

"Would you like to come and give me a cuddle?"

They had a nice long cuddle.

"Did you notice that horrid boy, Eric", said Richard, I saw him kissing Betsy under the table.

"Ooh! What shall we do to him?"

The next day, they cut out the words from a newspaper. "Alan Jones is f***ing Jill Bates". Two days later, Angela pushed an envelope under the headmistress's door. The word "Scandal!" was pasted on the envelope.

The local uproar that this caused entertained them hugely as they cuddled in bed that evening.

Richard had to move to a separate bedroom when they turned eleven. He and Angela would wait for their parents to come up to bed, normally around half-past ten. When Richard, who was nearer, heard one of them snoring, he came quietly across the passage to Angela's room. It was not long before they got to know each other more intimately. It was just exploratory at first.

"What's this little willie doing?" she said, "It's meant to get hard when I hold it".

"You just wait another year or two", he said, "but you can play with it if you like". She giggled, and they had fun.

St Martins, the boarding school where he had been a pupil, now took girls as well as boys, from the age of eleven. It was still seen as a very good school. The headmaster, Mr Hardy – known to the pupils as "flat arse" – remembered teaching their father all those years ago. He could see that Richard and Angela were marked out for the same distinction as their parent. The twins could not put a foot wrong.

They decided to do nothing untoward in their first year at St Martins. In their second year they amused themselves by setting fire to a storeroom, and leaving a trail of evidence pointing to a boy who fancied himself. And Richard, having locked a master in the lavatory one day, stood outside and played back a recording that Angela had made on her smart phone, of a boy shouting foul abuse at an unnamed person. The boy was expelled. Some of their acts of sabotage made headlines in the local paper, and one serious scandal led to a police investigation. Richard and Angela were thanked for "helping the police with their enquiries". On two occasions, their suggestions led to the conviction of a boy, and then a girl, that they disliked.

The transition to their teenage years was effected with ease and grace, raising their appeal to a new level. Richard stood out as taller and better looking than his contemporaries, and both of them excelled at sport and athletics. In their personal life, cuddling had developed into a more active form of enjoyment. He told Angela of his first wet dream. "About time", she said, and showed him what to do.

They were careful to avoid stirring envy and were modest about their successes. But one boy nursed a grievance. If it were not for those two, he thought, he would have been the one to stand out. He, Jasper Morland, would have been the one that Mr Hardy held up as a model for all to follow. He made the mistake of telling them, "You think you're so clever, don't you? but the only reason old flat-arse picks you out is because your dad was here. Otherwise you'd be nobodies".

They said nothing; they just looked at the wretched boy. He tried to make them angry, and they just looked at him. He walked away, feeling uneasy.

They gave this case their special attention. It would be the last one before settling down to serious work in their final term. The idea of torture, physical torture, came quickly. They had never gone this far before. It seemed especially fitting for Jasper, and they agreed on a suitable punishment. The boy was a keen runner, and had a particular route for his daily run before lunch. It was a track that went through woodland on the school's northern boundary, and they found the ideal spot to get him. Shortly after mid-day, they would be seen to leave the school grounds in another direction, then walk back to where they had planned their little action in the woods. After their attack, they would next be seen sauntering back into the school grounds at the same point. Hearing the boy's muffled screams, they would rush to his help.

It all went perfectly. They laid a narrow rope across the path, and then hid behind thick bushes. Angela pulled up the rope as Jasper passed; after running fast he fell heavily. Richard sprang out and flung himself along Jasper's body. His weight held the smaller boy down. Angela gave him a yellow duster to shove under Jasper's mouth. Then Angela gave him the first of three large, metal staples. Richard put it over the boy's neck and banged it into the ground with a mallet. He did the same with both legs. Jasper was unable to move. Angela then punctured him with a sharp knife in his thighs, his buttocks, and between his ribs, going far enough in to hurt, but not enough to cause real damage.

It had been done quietly, and Jasper would never know there had been two assailants. Strolling back a few moments later, they ran to where the muffled shouts were coming from. Richard yelled at Angela to get help. She found a master who came running, with others behind him.

The twins were praised for their presence of mind. Richard especially was the hero of the day. And again, they helped the police with their enquiries, describing as best they could the figure of a man they had seen coming out of the school grounds and running across the road into the woodland on the other side. The local paper noted that an escaped schizophrenic had been on the loose at the time of the attack. The case was never resolved.

They were among the first to visit Jasper in the school's sanatorium. They came with sympathy and a small box of chocolates. Jasper looked at them, shamefaced.

"I'm sorry I spoke to you as I did," he managed to say. He found apologies difficult. Angela said, "Don't give it another thought. We can be friends again. But tell us, what exactly happened to you?"

They listened, wide-eyed, while Jasper told them of the enormous monster who had held him down and then tortured him.

"Oh, that must have been awful!" Richard said, looking briefly at Angela. "You poor chap".

After leaving Jasper, Angela said, "I almost felt sorry for him".

"Well, he's still a bit of a creep. But I've been thinking. I don't want to do anything like that again. I think we pushed our luck too far … too much planning … people aren't worth it".

Four years later, Richard and Angela came down from Cambridge, each with a First in Mathematics. They had stopped sleeping with each other, having discovered the greater joys of falling in love in the normal way. They shared the same day for their weddings, and then produced children who looked set to be as beautiful and clever as their parents.

Their birthdays were close enough to be combined into one celebration; and the one for their sixth had special resonance for the parents. They smiled at each other, with remembered complicity. "We were awful, weren't we?" Angela said, and Richard replied, "Looking back, I suppose I should be ashamed of some of the things we did; but it was satisfying at the time. But, please God, let our children be innocent of all that".

They watched little Anna and Roderick, as they stood at the front door, shaking hands with the departing guests. A very old lady was bending over them, beaming. "Oh, what adorable little children! And you're just like your mother and father" she said. Anna and Roderick smiled back at her.

Richard shuddered. "Oh, the children, the children!"

"But are we happy or horrified to see history repeating itself?" Angela asked him.

He put it back to her, "Does it matter now?"

TWINS

W E ARE IDENTICAL twins. When we were eight, our mother sat us down one day and said, "Peter and Paul, you are clever boys. I can make you even cleverer, and successful. I have told you that I am a neurosurgeon and you understand quite well what that means. I have now perfected a new technique. I could change the wiring, the connections in your brains, so, in effect, I shall be planting cookies. They will give you a shared consciousness. Just imagine: each of you will know what the other is thinking. There will be no secrets between you. But you won't want secrets; it would be like keeping secrets from yourself. The two of you will be sharing the same mind. You will still see what is before your own eyes. It will be like it is now for anyone, and you can switch between the two views as you like. The difference is that this is what your shared mind will do, without special lenses."

We were dumbstruck. We just looked at her. She smiled and said, "You must not decide too quickly. You should think about it carefully, talk to each other and decide what questions to ask me. I'll wait for you to tell me when you're ready."

We thought of little else. We asked her a lot of questions. Mostly we liked the idea, but what were the risks? Would we inevitably cheat in school exams? If we went to university, could we do different subjects and learn them all equally? If one felt pain, would the other feel it? Could we make money out of it?

She answered each one.

"There are no risks to physical health; mental health might be a problem with less clever children, but it should be no problem for you two.

"With some questions, matter of fact ones, you either know the answer or you don't. Some questions require thinking, such as drawing distinctions, and others ask for your opinion on something. You would have to make sure you don't write exactly the same answer. They pick up on word-for-word copying because it means you've seen someone else's answer.

"It would be sensible to take different courses at university because, yes, you would learn each other's work. You couldn't expect to learn everything as thoroughly as the other, but that won't matter. You each retain what you have learnt separately, and you'll always have ready access to what the other has learnt. After a time, the two lots of knowledge will merge anyway.

"And yes, you would feel each other's pain. Some say it's good for you to share your suffering. Fellow feeling is good for us all. And think, there should be more pleasures for you to share than there are pains.

"Moneymaking? There would be possibilities. You'd be like the circus freaks we had when I was a child. You paid tuppence and got to see the three-legged woman. Not very nice. Is that what you want to do? You'll have to make up your minds when you're older. You could do great wrong, through greed for money, or an evil sense of humour. I know I can trust your sense of right and wrong. But remember! Till then you must let me guide you on questions of behaviour. What you must do now is think, long and hard. Do not rush it. Take it slowly, in stages."

In the end we decided to go ahead with it. It worked much as our clever mum had said it would. Sadly, she died quite soon after. And we thought of another question we should have asked her. The day came when we would find the answer, but by then it was too late.

With her death, there was an almighty scandal; "Two children brain-damaged deliberately by mad mother!" was one headline.

We were, you could say, in two minds over this. We were shocked by what mum had done; but we also admired her. We remembered how she had made sure that we first considered every aspect, and only then made our decision. We were questioned. Did we understand what she had done? What had she told us? Did we notice any difference before and after our operation? We did not let on that we knew well what she had done, but we would never tell them. The operating team that supported mum's surgery thought the purpose of the two operations was for something else entirely. She had told them it was something to do with a common fault in our neural networks. We pretended not to know the scientific words. They looked at the film record, but at the critical moments her hand had covered what she was doing. She was too clever for them.

An intelligent couple were chosen to adopt us. They were naturally inquisitive and asked a lot of questions, gently, of course, but persistent. We gave nothing away. We guarded what our mum had done. It was a trump card that we would never reveal.

When the time came and we were asked which universities appealed to us, we decided against it. Why bother? We left home and said goodbye to the couple who had adopted us. They had been kind, they had cared for us well. They had adopted us because they loved us and would continue to do so. We knew what love meant; we had observed it as a common aspect of being human. We saw it as alien to a life of the mind. But we did not want to make them unhappy; we promised to keep in touch, but could see they were disappointed and unhappy.

We of course were happy. This is what we had planned from the beginning. We were going off on our own, to wander, enjoy life, and make money.

We found several ways of doing this. We played as freaks on television, in a modern version of the three-legged woman. Good old mum. Imagine: one of us is in New York and the other in London. One appears to struggle to say what the other is doing: "I see him at a concert … yes … is it Bach? … and so on. "Fantastic feats of telepathy!" We made money very quickly.

To carry this off, we had to look different. So we have different hairstyles, and one of us uses a sunlamp for tanning. Our passports show us as different; and we wear different frames for our glasses.

It was a big moment when we married. Pamela and Penelope are identical twins. Like us, they dress differently, and do even more than we can with their hairstyles. Pamela is wife to Peter; Penelope is married to Paul. We laugh at our double bigamy and our nights of dual passion. We had to let our wives into the secret. They were thrilled and they understood it must remain secret among the four of us. And with marriage, we discovered the joys of sexual intercourse.

We could not play the same double act indefinitely. People might get suspicious, especially neurologists. Our case still puzzled them, but it was at least off the front pages. We performed our telepathy act where it might be less widely reported; and in some places, places in Africa for example, it showed that there was still magic in the world. Our act made less money there, but we must not be too greedy.

Another idea came to us. We loved music and were quite good pianists. It helped that we were well below the level for concert performers; we could perform at a more popular level and not attract wide comment. It was the mathematical side that we exploited. Dave Brubeck had made his name being able to count difficult time signatures, like 7/4 and 13/4. We did the same, and were liked for the way we could knock out complex and frequently changing cross-rhythms. The trick was for one of us to be seen doing this live, while the other was elsewhere. One would be counting one beat while the other counted the other one. Each would be aware of the two beats, so there was one performer and two brains controlling the rhythms. No one would guess how we did it.

Best of all was when we got jobs in separate banks. We could use information of what was going on in each other's bank. Insider trading, in effect, and we were rewarded for high performance. It was fool proof.

It came to a sudden end. One day, walking out of a shop, Pamela was disfigured by a lunatic throwing acid at her face. Peter was in such grief that I could not bear it. And shortly after, I saw him looking at my wife, Penelope. Please note, I no longer write "we". I am I and he is he. The cookies have crumbled. Passion, jealousy and rage were beyond our brains' ability to handle. When I saw the lust in his eyes, looking at Penelope, I knew this was not just an intellectual problem. We were in the grip of violent emotions, like being invaded by aliens.

Peter and I made our peace. Our wives have left us, and I can't say I blame them. We were coming to recognize a lot of strange things about the way people live. It was the question we had never thought to ask our mum. We had now found the answer the hard way. What it means to be human. We had discovered the 'human condition'.

THE VILLAGE OF WIDOWS

W E LOVED this village, Justin and I, the moment we saw it. We had been looking for our place of retirement, and this was it. We were very happy here.

Our son, and only child, was working in America, and when the time came he would retire there with his American wife. We visited them there, perhaps two or three times a year; we noticed our two grandsons getting bigger and brighter every time and wished we could come more often. And the family came to us too seldom; it was difficult for them, with the children. So it's not ideal, but many families live this way now. Justin and I wanted the quieter life, here in England. Sadly he died too soon to enjoy it. I found I had joined the generation of widows. But I found, too, that this was a good place for a widow; and when the time came, it would be a good place to die.

Everyone has to accept the challenges of retirement; and widowhood raises greater ones. But I remembered my mother used to say, "There isn't a cloud without its silver lining". She was an inspiring example. When she had finished grieving for Dad, she discovered a new life. She had a new sense of liberation. She was free at last from the old duties, the housework and the caring, the scrubbing and fetching and carrying. Now she could choose what to do and when to do it. I would follow my mum's example.

Socially, Little Hatchet has suited me well. The ranks of widows seems to grow year by year, by one, two, and sometimes three – faster than they drop off at the other end. It creates a bond between us. But it's not just us single women. If you walk down the main street here, at most times of the day, there is usually someone you know to stop for a chat. You will soon be taking morning coffee together; then you have little lunch parties at home; and in this way everyone gets to know everyone they would want to know. The last step is the dinner party, with candles, good wine and family cutlery. And that is how I met Arthur Manning, at Sheila Collingwood's dinner party last year.

It was a good party. Sheila is a splendid cook and she and her husband are good hosts; everyone is drawn into the conversation. Someone that evening raised the subject of retirement. Sheila started,

"I think you see two types, don't you? There are the ones who want to forget about their past work-a-day jobs, and all that effort, keeping at it to save up for a comfortable retirement – something you've not chosen from a sense of vocation. Then there are the ones who naturally retain an interest in their past career. Look at Jack Compton: an ex-surgeon at the top of his profession when he retired. Arthur, where do you come in this; which sort are you?"

"Oh, very much the former. I was in the import–export business. I spent a lot of time in Poland, and, I don't know if I've mentioned, but I married a Polish woman I met. We had a very happy life there – until my wife died, from a heart attack". He paused. Mary Johnson filled the gap, "That must have been awful for you, Arthur. You know what we call this place? The village of widows. I think villages like this are a natural home for them.

But you're special, as a widower. Rose," she said, turning to me, "Arthur does the most amazing job here. He has a little group of widows that he keeps happy – I'm one of them ... now no blushes and modesty, Arthur, you're a godsend. Rose, he takes each of us in turn, once a week, for an outing in his lovely car; and every four weeks we go round for tea and cakes, and draw up a programme for the next four weeks."

"Yes, Arthur, a lot of us here know what a good job you do." Another guest intervened, "I agree; but talking of Poland ..." The conversation moved on, seldom lagging for more than a moment.

I went home thinking this really was a good place to live. And Arthur looked nice.

I bumped into him one morning, shortly after. We stood and chatted for a while, saying what a pleasant evening it had been, and wasn't the food wonderful, and so on. Then he said, "Mary told you about our little widows' group; what she didn't tell you is that we like to keep one or two as back-ups in case of absence. It occurred to me that you might like to be one. Would you like to think about it?"

He told me the names of the other three, and to take my time in deciding. I made up my mind on the spot, but I never like to sound too eager. I rang him a couple of days later and said I would be happy to go on his list, and come on outings with him when convenient. He thanked me and said he would tell the others.

Life looked up.

During the next couple of months Arthur called on me twice. It was fun. Then he rang again, a few weeks later.

"Rose, I expect you saw that Mary died last week ... drowned on a holiday ... absolute tragedy ... so young ... and such a lovely woman. We shall miss her dreadfully. So. We want to keep things going. Would you like to join us full time? I've asked the others, and they all said you'd be perfect. We've just come to the end of a month and we're having a month off, out of respect – I'm sure you'll understand. And then we gather again on Thursday the twenty-first for the usual tea and cakes at my house. Would that be all right with you?"

I expressed my own shock and sadness at the news; and said I'd be happy to join them full time.

After a few weeks I was well into the routine. And I had been doing some research. I was curious about this good-looking young widower. He looked no more than his early sixties. A normal man in his position, with all his advantages, would have taken a new wife long before now. God's gift to widows, you might say. He had been running this little group for three or four years. Each of us four women was marriageable, in our individual way. We were reasonably attractive – especially, I have to say, myself. So was he a catch to pursue? Or just someone to play with?

You can find out a lot about someone by chatting to friends and neighbours. People love to gossip, as long as it's not too obvious. And then there's Google on the computer. I confess I am something of a snooper. I even searched out old newspaper clippings.

Arthur Manning had had a good career in the export–import business. He would have left with a good pension and a tidy sum put away. You could see it in his house, tastefully furnished and lots of well-chosen pictures and objets d'art scattered about. From the beginning I had seen him as a prospective husband, though it was clear he did not see me in that way. There was nothing to suggest he had had other than a normally happy marriage – but then I found a small mention in the local paper of where he had kept a small home in England; his principal residence being in Warsaw. Ten years ago, his wife had divorced him, on grounds of serial adultery. This gave me something to think about.

And it posed a challenge greater than I had bargained for. Did I still want it? What if he played fast and loose with me? He might have grown out of it – but who knew what he did on those trips to London? Well, if it's just a matter of being a naughty boy once a week, it would take the strain off me. Was I in love with Arthur? Of course not; I liked him a lot, and saw no reason why there should not be mutual affection. He was good company. I knew I would never fall in love again, not at my age. He must feel the same. I admired his status and the achievements of a professional life well spent. More to the point, he was a very attractive man with a very nice home, way beyond what my first husband could have afforded. What could go wrong?

I laid my plans.

Arthur made it clear to his widows – and I got the message on our first outing together, that we should not bring up anything personal about our past romantic life. It was his philosophy, he said, that a widow should start a new life. Forget the past; think only of the future.

I waited a few weeks before making a move. We had had a good afternoon out in the country; now we were lingering over tea and scones. He looked at his watch.

"Arthur", I said, "you recognise children as an indelible link to the past, so how can we forget anything so important in our past?"

"Oh there are many parts of one's life that make us the person we are. Of course. It's our past absorption in the late partner that we should overcome. Not forget, never forget; but it is wrong to spend the last years of one's life in permanent regret, looking back, when we should be looking forward to a few more years of happiness."

"Until the ravages of time take their toll", I added.

"Yes, but just look at you ladies, all in very fine fettle. There's a lot to look forward to."

"I get the impression that you may be the youngest of us. And what you do for us is a great kindness."

I put my finger briefly on the arm that he had rested on the table.

"I do it because I enjoy it", he said.

"I know you want to avoid intimacy, but I tell you, I wonder why someone as young, attractive and interesting as you are, can have remained unhooked. Forgive me. This is all too personal, but I wanted to get it off my chest."

I think he blushed a little. He looked down, silent for a while, gave a rueful smile and said, "you do go too far, but your compliment is appreciated. Perhaps I'll tell you one day."

This was the moment to tell my big lie.

"Arthur, I think you must have suffered enough in your life. I don't know if I should tell you, but I was overcome with sorrow last week. I was in London for the day, and bumped into a very old friend from way back". I let my hand rest on his arm.

"I told her about this wonderful group I had joined, and I

mentioned your name and sang your praises. She was surprised. She knew you, when you lived up north. Among the many good things she said about you was how sad it was for everyone when you and Ellen parted ..."

Arthur went rigid. I removed my hand from his arm.

"Oh my dear, I'm so sorry. It must still be very painful."

We sat silently for a while. I continued, "Can I say something? I want to help you. It seems to me that it's you that needs looking after. You would benefit so much from having someone to live with. You could just take your pick, you know? Really!" I gave an embarrassed laugh. "For Heaven's sake, I'm not pushing myself. I'm not the type to remarry."

He looked at his watch. "Time to go", he said bleakly.

In the car, going back, I waited for him to speak. He pulled into the first lay-by.

"Rose, you've touched a very sore point. I shall think of what you've told me. But we must all go on as before. I've been living here under a lie, haven't I? I had to. For me, it was a way of getting over the whole messy business of that divorce. And it gives me a sense of atonement, making my four widows happy. I'd have lost all credibility if they found out. You see that, don't you? You'll keep my secret?"

"Of course I will, Arthur. I'm not one to moralise."

He put his hand briefly on my lap. It was well after six when we got back.

I was on my way!

We thought we should avoid meeting, to avoid gossip. We talked a lot on the phone, and be frank with each other. He told me his feeling for me had been growing. I sensed that he was getting fond of me, and I nursed him along the way to telling me that it was becoming serious. And the breakthrough came.

"Rose, I think love might come. I hope you feel the same way. I mustn't deceive you. We must both be sure. I'm wondering … I shall have to leave here anyway … could we have two weeks somewhere … to see if we could make a go of it?"

I was home and dry. I said of course. We must both be quite, quite certain. And he could rely on me to handle my own, separate departure. We would meet up that night at the hotel he had chosen, deep in Wales.

I knew what to expect when the five of us met for the last time, when he would tell them he had to leave Little Hatchet.

"There's something I have to tell you", he said, after the tea and cakes. "It's been on my mind for some time. I've had a yearning to go back to my roots in the north. While I'm still young enough. I must make a new start. I've put this house on the market and I'll be moving soon. It's very sad to say goodbye, but it's better to have a quick, clean break. It's been a wonderful four years for me; we've had so much fun and I shall miss you all … have wonderful memories of our time together."

It was a bit of a bombshell for the others. They had a lot to say how much they'd loved it and could never forget him. I said my bit, as the other three had. Arthur handled it well. They were all very sad. They wished him future happiness, And that was it.

The time came for him to stand up; and time for us to go. He went to open the front door for us. As the others filed past him, each embraced him and exchanged kisses. I was the last. I stood there chatting, long enough for the others to disperse. Then I smiled at him, "at last, my darling. Just you and me. I'm already packed."

"I'm sorry, Rose", he said, "it's not going to work, is it? We have no future together."

He held out his hand but I didn't shake it. I was stunned.

"You set me up, didn't you? You just played me along! Bastard!" I shouted.

GOD KNOWS WHY

I T is one minute to midnight in the White House.

Trrring, trrring; trrring, trrring; trrring.

"Hello. You are through to the White House. Be aware that this call will be recorded for reasons of national security. Please select one of the following four options:

– to hear the President read his morning prayer, press 1;

– to listen to the testimonials of support for the President's – work, from religious, commercial and community leaders, press 2;

– to speak to a member of the White House staff, press 3;

– to speak to the President, please hold.

The Four Seasons is heard. And then a Voice.

"Oh, Me! Oh Holy Me! I wish I'd found another job for that Vivaldi fellow."

The White House switchboard begins to shake and rattle.

Another voice is heard.

"Hello, hello," irritably, "who is that calling, please?"

"This is God."

"God? God! What do you want, God?"

"I want to speak to President George W. Bush."

"Please hold. I'll see if he's in."

A lengthy pause is filled with Elvis Presley singing *Shake, Rattle and Roll*. This is interspersed with "Thank you for holding. Your call is important to us. We will answer soonest."

"Hello, God. You still there?"

"I'm always here."

"The President is presently tied up at this time. He's on another line, talking to Mr Blair. Mr Blair is the British Prime Minister."

"I know who Mr Blair is. He calls me every morning. It's Mr Bush I want to talk to. I've been trying to get him all week."

"Will you hold? Or will you call back later?"

"Tell Mr Bush from me that if he doesn't come to the phone right away, I'll personally see him in Hell."

"Okay, God, okay, okay. I'll do my best."

A short pause is filled with Bob Dylan singing *God Knows*.

"Hi God! George here. How ya doin'? Sorry about this telephone system, I need new equipment. Now, what can I do for you?"

"It's more a question of what I can do for you. Don't you want my support for some military adventure?"

"Sure do, God, sure do. This guy Saddam has to go. He's evil. I'd like to have you on my side, and of course I'm sure you are, but – you know – I'd like to have a special message from you that I can pass on to the folks down here."

"Going to war is itself an evil thing, Mr President."

"Oh sure God, sure, but it's a necessary evil in this instance. It's the only way to secure a God-given democracy in the Middle East. Besides, if you don't support me, millions of God-fearing American people, who think you're a regular guy, will start to wonder. I'd have to think very seriously about all the support I've been giving to the churches in God's own country. You know what I'm saying, God? Either you're with me or you're against me."

God pauses. There is the faint sound of a celestial choir in the background.

"Well, if you put it like that, Mr President, you'd better go ahead. But make a good clean job of it."

"Will do, God, will do. Now you take care, ya hear me? And my best wishes to that fine boy of yours and his lovely mother. Oh, and I'll pass you to my assistant here. She'll give you my private number. Bye, 'n' God bless."

INNOCENCE

THIS IS a nice town. People smile at you when they pass you in the street. If the smile lingers, the next to pass, seeing your smile, will smile at you. I have often played with the idea that if sufficient numbers were to come and go, and with the right spacing between them, one might see a Mexican wave of smiles rippling down the street one side and up the other. One day, seeing a lovely girl smiling at me, I stopped and asked her,

"Don't I know you?"– knowing quite well that I didn't.

She stopped. I saw her thinking and saw that she was glad to be asked.

"Where might that have been?"

"Ah! I wonder if it was in Umbria last year."

A more personal smile now, looking straight at me.

"I have never been to Umbria."

"Oh but you must go! It's enchanting. So much to do and so few people to spoil the view."

"It sounds just what I like."

I looked at my watch, as though wondering whether I had time to spare.

"Well, if you can find the time I'd be happy to tell you more about it. When I coffee in town, I go to Mollie's."

And that's how it started. Easy.

We were soon seeing each other often. At first, she, being modest, left it to me to suggest things to do. It was not long before we were inviting each other home, she to my flat, and I to her small terraced house. She had a nice little garden at the back with a small private space where she could sit or lie unobserved. I came one day, unannounced, through her unlocked door. I saw her – and this is how I shall remember her – she was sitting in the lotus position, in her own private space. A meditative smile played on her face, glowing softly. She looked as though she had just been deliciously, luxuriantly penetrated. Was I the one she had seen loving her in that way? If she were a cat she would be purring. She saw me now and came back to the world.

"Chris! What a lovely surprise! I was just thinking of you," she said, and coloured prettily.

"Well, I'm flattered. You looked so happy. Content with life. Sorry to surprise you like that but your front door was unlocked. Again! You must take care. Anyone could just walk in."

"I'm glad you did."

I knelt beside her. I stroked her back.

"Juliet, the innocent maiden. So trusting, so lovely, so adorable," I murmured; then whispered in her ear, "and waiting to be ravished?"

We went indoors.

I like innocence. I like innocent women. I should not like to be innocent myself; it would spoil so much of the fun in life. A worldly woman would see right through me, and where's the fun in that.

This is a boring town. I woke one morning in a foul mood.

This affair had been running too long. And so, walking down the street, I had a fixed scowl on my face. If I looked at passers-by, they scowled back. And I played with the idea that if sufficient numbers were to come and go, and with the right spacing between them, one might see a Mexican wave of scowls rippling down this street and up the other. The thought of it gave me grim satisfaction and I scowled some more. But when a lovely girl stopped and scowled back, I also stopped.

"Why were you scowling at me?"

"I'm sorry. I woke up in a foul mood this morning. I just can't shake it off. Perhaps you could help me."

"How could I do that, supposing I wanted to?"

"When I'm in town, feeling like this, I go to Mollie's for a coffee. And I would like to apologise to you." I gave her a small smile, and added "they have lovely cakes there."

She took her time in replying.

"All right then, but I can't stay long."

I brought the coffees to the table, sat down and said,

"Don't I know you?" – knowing quite well that I didn't.

"Where might that have been?"

"Ah! I wonder if it was in Umbria, last year."

"I have never been to Umbria."

"Oh but you must go! It's enchanting. So much to do and so few people to spoil the view."

"Sounds all right."

Well, the details were different, but the affair followed a similar pattern. Her name was Gudrun – the best thing about her. If I saw Juliet in the street, I made sure she didn't see me, especially if I was with Gudrun. She had kicked up an awful fuss when I walked out on her. I would not want her telling Gudrun what she thought of me.

But after all, this is the best, most wonderful town I could imagine. It is the right size to have good friends and neighbours that one sees when one likes, while remaining anonymous to everyone else. It's a good town to live and to work in, and – who knows? – one day a good town to die in. When I walk into shops, the men nod at me and the women smile. I have a job I love. I teach Geography in the local comprehensive. The school has a good reputation. I enjoy seeing the boys and girls in my class look up at me. Some may become friends, as I became friends with some of those who taught me – I see them in the street; we may have a drink or drop into a pub for lunch. Some of the girls I teach are quite pretty but I have no urge to see them after school. Some have tried but I like my women when they have started to mature and beginning to get the used look, while still innocent enough not to see through me.

I know I shall want to settle down with someone I love and live with till death us do part. But there are still wild oats to be sown – knowing full well that it could ruin my chances if I get a bad reputation. St Augustine put it nicely. Oh, Lord, make me cease from my philandering – but not yet.

Oh, God, what a bore.

THE JOURNEY

A life sentence in 500 words

HALVARD REMEMBERS sitting in the pushchair with his mother smiling down at him as she wheels him through the park all green the grass the leaves on the trees and a blue sky above and he remembers sitting in the back of a car in his own little seat, Hal's special seat Mummy calls it and he loves the motion and the trees again the trees that flash past the car window with the blue sky above but now he is in the back as they drive him to a school far from home with the sky grey and the rain falling but in just a few years he is driving himself which he loves when a girl sits beside him and he has his first kiss with Jean, on the back seat, and then there are others so many that it is hard to remember all their names now and all the loving them and leaving them but now it is Deborah who sits there his first proper girlfriend one he can imagine being beside him for always but after a time he asks himself do I want to go through life with this same girl chattering idly about nothing much and so it goes on he is never quite sure who it should be until it is Gudrun who comes some of the way with him then it is Belle beautiful Belle who gives him the comforting feel of her hand on his thigh while he drives and he loves her hand resting there but better still when it is Rosemary's hand because it is she who will become his wife and she tells him it would be unfair to leave her at home while he drives to work so he marries Hilary who loves to be there for him when he comes home and one day he puts her hand on his thigh and she gives it a squeeze of love and it is like that for some years until their divorce sends them on separate ways sad they had no children but now it is Virginia sitting beside him so utterly sweet so charming and chatting so gaily about their journey together and all the things in their wonderful life and so much still lying in store for them and so they go ever onward until it is he who is the passenger sitting next to Virginia yes it is still Virginia who is driving and he sits beside her resting his hand on her thigh as they approach the end of their journey but when the girl tells them they have reached their destination they laugh calling it premature but one day when they stop, Virginia gets the wheel chair for Hal and she is pushing him right up to the end when all that remains is the final journey he in his long gleaming box with bright brass handles and her looking down at him before she starts on her own final journey alone.

NATHAN

NATHAN always had to have his own way. From the age of seven, by guile or deceit or by sheer force of will, he must get what he wanted. It was not toys, not sweets nor presents that he craved. He wanted the sense of achievement, of having met the goals he had set for himself. He wanted to be top dog among his peers. By sheer force of will he would overcome all opposition; and it got him further in life than anyone could have imagined. Once, he came crashing down, hard. But that was another challenge. He met it and conquered it, not caring about collateral damage. And only he could have done it. So he finished on top, in one sense. But as a man, not just a tycoon, it was the bottom. And he was alone. All alone.

It started in a small way. His parents had come to this little village in Derbyshire, to buy the village shop. They never regretted it, and when their time came, they were buried in the churchyard nearby. Their little shop sold newspapers, groceries, and a miscellaneous variety of household goods. They called themselves Mum and Dad, after Nathan was born. A lovely couple, the villagers called them, and in their last years they were the Derby and Joan.

Nathan was a lovely boy and it was not long before they could see that he was clever, much cleverer than either of them. They talked proudly of his probable future. They wondered if he might one day leave this lovely corner of Derbyshire, a countryside still blessed with peace in an ever noisier world, with the hills, the valleys, the streams and the walks that were there for their Sundays and holidays. They would walk, sun or shine. Soon after he was born, Nathan joined them, carried by his father in a pouch held on his chest. When he was big enough they used a folding pushchair, keeping to the paths; and the next stage had little Nathan scrambling around on his own. He was totally fearless and needed careful watching. As an older boy he would walk on his own. He loved the feeling of independence, up on the hills. He would set himself ever harder tasks, to go further and higher. His physical fitness was one of his great assets, and when he grew up it would make him noticeable. Women admired the power and the strength of the man; the power of his will and determination that one could see in his eyes and jaw.

From the age of six, Nathan had wanted to help in the shop. He liked it better than he liked schooling. His father told him he must learn to read and write, if nothing else. All the other stuff would follow. He must be able to understand others, and make himself understood to them. And he must get his sums right, be quick at mental arithmetic and feel comfortable with numbers. His father, of course, was looking ahead but Nathan got there first. In his last year at the village primary school and long before most boys his age even knew what the words meant, he had developed a grasp of big numbers, of risks and probabilities. It was the foundation of his rapid rise to wealth and power.

By the time he was eleven, his father could trust him with the till. Young Nathan saw which lines were making the most money. Before coming home from school in the nearby town he went first into other stores like his father's but bigger. He saw the ways that goods were displayed; he saw how the little luxuries, the "treats", were placed close to the till, and understood the psychology of impulse buying. By the time he left school he had doubled his father's turnover. Customers were coming from far around.

"We've done well, Dad", he said.

"Thanks to you, son"; and he added in the age-old way, "this'll all be yours one day".

"Dad, I talked to the manager at Madison's, on my way home this afternoon. He's given me a job. I start on the first of next month."

"You've done what? And not talked to us first? I'd no idea you were thinking on those lines. What do you think Mum will say?"

But this was to be the way Nathan did things. He had his objective, and went straight at it.

In fact, it was what his father had long had to recognise as a likely possibility. A lad with his qualities, you had to expect it. But it was sudden, and he so young. Mum would not like it. The three of them had been a close family, working together, sitting and eating together. They went walking and watched the telly together. It was going to make a big change to their lives. Still, the nearby town was not far away. They would see him often. It was where he had gone to school and it was a good place to work. It is what boys did. They grew up and they left home. And sometimes went far away.

Nathan had learnt the essentials at school. Not just English and arithmetic, but also how to handle people. He saw teachers melt when he smiled at them. He had a group of boys around him, ones he had picked. Those he did not want he kept at a distance. It was his manipulation of people that was one of his greatest assets. An astute observer would have seen how he used others to help him, willingly and unwittingly. They could see that their friend Nathan was the right type. He was kind, a real friend. But for Nathan emotion played no part. Being kind and generous, being a good friend to the right people, was a card he played. The truth was, he didn't give a toss about them as people, just so long as they did what he wanted. They had never seen the warm eyes snap cold shut when he turned his head away.

It was different with his parents. A special warmth would always remain for them, his mum and dad; they had given him everything a child could reasonably want. He thought this must be love; and he thought this was a love that mattered. He knew that in many ways he had exceeded his parents' expectations, without their understanding how he had got on in the world. It did not matter. They were the two people he would never want to manipulate to his own ends. At the table and on the walks, it was the easy talking that gave him his bedrock for life, and was the crucible of his ambition. His mum and dad encouraged him; they admired him as much as they loved him. He would always remember it, a warm thought for a cold man to carry.

The manager at Madison's quickly saw the talent in the new young man. Madison's was one of a chain, and inside of fifteen months Nathan was picked out for management training. After that his career in retail took off. At the age of twenty-five he was managing one of their prime stores, in a Midlands city. He learnt quickly, testing the lines of merchandise to be stocked, and finding ways to improve staff performance. He made few friends and not a few enemies; he knew it, but it did not bother him. He had read many books on how to get to the top. That was his aim and he knew he could do it. He was relentless. By his early thirties he was on the board of a larger competitor. He had seen the weak spots in Madison's, and led a successful take over of his old firm. He went straight to the board as a director of the new one. But why stick at retail? The money was coming in and banks were competing for his custom. He bought real estate, manufacturing firms and parts of the travel industry. He invested widely and well. Debt was essential, but he was clever in varying its sources and controlling its level.

So we find him, at thirty-five, rich, successful and well regarded in the higher circles of commerce and finance. There was a presence to him. He was tall, well built, and immaculately tailored. Women found him attractive. It was time to start a private life.

He needed a wife to be seen standing by his side, meeting government ministers at dinner, and captains of industry at banquets. She would have to be attractive, more than just a token wife. He wanted a woman with a keen sense of business, who would understand what he was doing, a wife who would accept his long hours of work and the days away on business, often abroad. Better if she were useful in his organisation, keeping an eye on manager's performance. Best of all if she had the initiative to expand the range and activities of his group.

He had been hiring women from an agency, when he needed one. They served an additional purpose afterwards if he wanted it. He had a list of those he could use again and picked out the ones who had showed a good sense of business. Then he threw it away. He did not want a re-tread. He went to a new agency and made a short list of four women. He took them in turn for dinner at an expensive restaurant. And so he finished with Laura. She was twenty-six, tall, slender and beautiful. She had a burning ambition to succeed in business. She had read many of the books that Nathan had read, and she seemed to like him. She was the prefect match.

He knew it was proper to have a wooing period. He made a point of being charming to her whenever they met. He paid her compliments, he smiled and attended to what she said. On the fourth occasion he took her home to his apartment for a drink, and asked her to marry him. She accepted; he was careful to conceal his lack of surprise. Two weeks later he gave himself two weeks leave. They got married at a registry office. Laura's parents hosted them well in the grounds of a castle, near the family home in Yorkshire. Her parents would pay for it, but he did politely offer to buy the champagne and the fine wines. His first invitation was to his Mum and Dad. Apart from them, there was no one that was important in his private life – he had never had much time for it. He invited some senior executives from other companies, men that he wanted to get to know better – thinking there might be a chance of doing business. In fact, there were not that many people from either side. Nathan had invited a journalist, who he introduced as a friend, and the journalist's cameraman was introduced as the wedding photographer. The next day the financial pages of the press carried photos of "The rising star of the boardrooms, with his lovely wife-to-be, Laura Pantolfe". The next day, a lesser paper showed a cartoon headed "The rising star of boardrooms (and bedrooms?" No, the lawyers stopped that one.

The wedding had gone well. Laura's parents made it a great occasion. They were happy to see their daughter marry money. Nathan made a point of introducing Mum and Dad to everyone – they were bewildered, but full of joy and pride, to see how well he had done, and he wanted to show he was as proud of them as they were of him.

It had not been easy for Nathan to choose a best man; he needed someone who could stand up and make jokes about him. No one had ever done that. But there was a senior colleague from work, who sat on two of the same company boards as Nathan. They often had a drink or two after the board meetings, joked a bit and quietly sized each other up. They had an extra drink one evening, and his colleague said he would do the job. They would each look up some good jokes.

"Don't worry Nat, it'll be all right on the night".

He did the job of best man quite well. The guests had had a few drinks by then and would have laughed at anything. So all went well on the night. After the champagne and confetti, the happy couple set off on their honeymoon. They would visit Paris, Rome, Stockholm and Madrid.

Nathan had never been so happy. He did not have to pretend; he found the words of love falling off his lips in unstoppable flow. On that first, wonderful night in Paris, they lay between the pink sheets in the opulent bed of the honeymoon suite. There were little putti cavorting across the elaborately carved headboard, and the nursery-style-erotic of Boucher reproductions hung on the walls behind them. Nathan did not notice them. He just saw Laura, his hands roamed all over her body, he was in a pink film of bliss. He said it had come on the wings of angels.

"Laura, my darling, lovely, lovely Laura, you are mine, only mine and I am hopelessly in love with you".

"Nathan, sweet Nathan, there could be no other husband," and she covered his face with kisses.

The next morning they took in the sights of Paris, the city of love. They went first to the ground floor of a large department store – three more were on their list that day. "You see where they put the ladies' cosmetics?" Laura said, "nothing leads you to them, you have to find your own way round. Where are the staff to help people? I'd make a much better job of it than this."

Nathan was thrilled to hear her talking like this. She's a clever woman, he told himself, and looked forward to telling his colleagues. And so the day progressed. It might be Nathan, it might be Laura, one or other would start the discussion on how to do things better, what layouts and stock lines would make a happier shopping experience for the customer. They had a lot to talk about at dinner that night, and again after their lovemaking. Money and sex; a potent cocktail.

"Tomorrow, we'll take in the boutique jewellers", Nathan said.

"Darling", Laura murmured.

"And we must see some of the other stuff, people will expect to see us as human. You know, the Eiffel Tower, Notre Dame; and we'll get seats for the opera."

The next morning, Nathan lavished jewels on Laura, telling her to pick out the best.

All this in two days! And Rome, Stockholm and Madrid lay ahead of them.

Home at last, in Nathan's Mayfair apartment, unpacked, showered and ready to eat, Nathan called up for supper in their dining room. The trolley came up, the waiter laid the table, uncovered and served the hot dishes, and covered the dessert to keep cool. Then, hand behind back, he poured the champagne, placed the red wine in a coaster, bowed and made his respectful exit.

They were relaxed in each other's company.

Nathan said, "I suppose you could call it a busman's honeymoon?"

They laughed, and Laura added, "that must make me the conductress who sells us the tickets".

"I'd buy the bus for you, my darling, I'd buy the whole company. But look, we're tired. It's been a wonderful two weeks. We've done a lot and now we should make an early night of it. I'll go into the office tomorrow, keep up to date with things, it shouldn't take long. I had my daily session with them on our trip. You could make an outline draft of what we should be planning for over the next few months.

They slept well that night, and had breakfast together the next morning, as working couples do.

Life and work went happily on. Laura learnt quickly and was soon indispensable to Nathan. She kept her eye on the inner workings of the Group, leaving him with more time to work on strategy; and she had ideas about the investment opportunities of the day.

"Nathan, this has to be good," she said one day. "It's worth two point eight billion, and you could get it for two point five. Easy. Read this and talk to them."

"I've been following this one for some time. You think now is the time? We're already overstretched, you know".

"Yes, but this is the big one. We can do a quick clean up and sell it on nine months later for half as much again. It'll more than cover our debts".

Nathan paused. Looked out the window.

He nodded.

"I'll do it."

It was unfortunate timing. Equity markets worldwide collapsed and the Nathan Group went to the wall. It had a personal and financial impact on Nathan. He was white with rage. He said not a word to Laura. He just looked at her. She paled and was silent. She would never forget that look, or the way that he then turned his back on her.

"It's going to take time to get over this."

"Darling, what can I say?"

"Best say nothing. I went along with it, all too willingly."

Over the next week, they slept back to back. After a silent breakfast, Nathan spoke.

"It's been difficult, hasn't it?"

"Yes, it hit both of us."

"What do you think we should do?"

Nathan was troubled. There had been moments in his life when the had felt he was slipping into, irrationality? He wondered now if this was another attack. He said nothing to Laura; she must never see him this way. It had been in the back of his mind that marriage would cure it. Evidently not.

He went to the office to begin the business of rescuing what he could and laying down a plan for the siege ahead. It was difficult to concentrate. He was smouldering with humiliation. And he would have to get used to living on a smaller income.

Four years or more of attrition left Nathan a changed man. In the course of his rise to wealth and power, he had survived minor setbacks, as every entrepreneur must. They had strengthened him. This last one had broken him. He seldom thought of Laura now. He had drifted away some time ago. How would he look at her now? He had worried about it, and still did, though not as much as he should have done.

It had been a month or two before he could visit his father. Now a widower, his father was not in good health. Nathan brushed aside his own troubles and kept the talk on his father's health. Two months later, Nathan was the chief mourner at his Dad's funeral.

He stood at the graveside and threw a handful of earth onto the coffin. The sound of it falling on the brown box brought a tear to his eye. He put a hand to his face to stop the sobs swelling inside him. As the mourners started filing away, the elderly vicar put a hand on his shoulder.

"It comes hard, my son. Only Christ can help you. Pray, and wait for God's solace".

The words remained with him. He wandered into his local church. He remembered as a boy, going with his mother on Sunday mornings. It was a habit he had dropped by the time he left home. Making money had been his only occupation. Sundays were a day of partial rest, a day of reckoning to reflect on the past week's performance. It was when he did his exercise of half an hour's power walking. In those days before the crash, it was business that occupied his mind. All that now meant less. The zest had gone. He knew he should attend to the markets. Even sitting here in church he thought of it but the stuffing had been knocked out of him. Failure occupied his consciousness. Sitting there in a pew, he sensed the presence of a man standing beside him. He stood up.

"Vicar, I hope you can help me. I have buried my father and grieve for him. I look back on my life and think I must have taken a wrong turning somewhere".

The story came out. The priest repeated the injunction to pray. Over the days ahead, Nathan came back to him and was affected by the man's fervour, his evangelism. Pray and make restitution, he said, you shall be saved by your good works. It came down to how much Nathan could afford. A sum was agreed. Nathan felt on home ground again. He applied himself to a portfolio of ethical investments for the church. The priest said to pay the money into the special account that he used on behalf of the church. They were small amounts at first, small in relation to Nathan's past scale of things, and it gave him a sense of control over his reverend friend. The markets had turned at last and Nathan's confidence rose in tandem.

And so the wheel of fortune came round again. It gave him a fresh start. But Nathan had changed. What was once a mere indifference to others was now an active repulsion from almost everyone. He wanted a minimum of contact with people, other than the domestic staff who provided for his domestic needs. One day, the priest came to him again – the portfolio was not doing well, the fabric of the building needed extensive work as a matter of urgency. Nathan turned a cold eye him.

"You've had enough from me. My money went into your personal account, didn't it? Don't bother me again."

He became richer than ever. But what was he to do with it? Had he ever been happy? It no longer made sense, making money was a way to be happy.

But he was not happy now. He could now live comfortably on the interest of his income. The question came back. What should he do with it? It was a question that came from the past and was not worth thinking about.

His disconnection from the world was getting worse. He was going mad. He stopped shaving. He bought some old clothes from a charity shop. He was given a dog at a foundling home and sat on the pavement outside a shop that he had once owned. He had a cloth cap that he placed on the pavement, with a scattering of coins in it. He liked to hear more coins falling on them. Why work for money when you could get people to give it to you? He no longer wanted the bother of buying and selling. He no longer studied the markets. Let others do all that tiresome stuff.

He was sitting there one day when Laura came up. She stopped in amazement.

"Nathan, darling, I've spent years wondering how to get hold of you. Where have you been? Why are you sitting like this on he pavement? You can't be poor."

"Don't just stand there. Give me some money".

Some things came back to him. He had loved her, once. What was she doing now, fiddling in her purse?

"Look, I'll give you what I've got on me, and I'm calling for an ambulance now. The ambulance was there a few minutes later. Laura had a word with them and they took him off to Accident and Emergency. He escaped as soon as he could.

Time passed. Why bother to sit outside on a pavement? He gave the dog back. He spent a few hundred million to build himself a bigger house. He had read that people like him had a swimming pool and a cinema. So that is what he must have. He never used them and there was no one to invite anyway. He spoke only to his staff. There were six, three men and three women. One of them was able to overcome her disgust of him sufficiently to go to his bed; he disgusted her and she demanded a large payment. Every day and all night he stayed at home. His staff ordered his provisions online. His wine cellar grew faster than he could drink it. He had been proud to have cases of the world's great vintages; and he had drunk them for want of anything better to do. His staff now drank them. One day he told his staff to disappear for a week. He passed the day drinking cheap wine and watching pornographic films. It was the nearest he got to remembering Laura.

At some time that night, he closed his eyes and saw the hills of Derbyshire. He had failed at love with a woman but there was still the memory of his Mum and Dad. He was walking with them on the peaks. The sun shone, the muted greens stretched out before him and there were puffy, white clouds in the blue sky. Tears fell from his eyes.

They found him the next morning. The postman had raised the alarm when the doorbell went unanswered. He needed a signature for the package that he brought every week. Nathan was on the floor. An empty bottle of cheap plonk lay beside him. Nathan was face down in his own vomit. The television was playing an endless loop of pornographic videos. A new one had come in that morning's package.

THE VICTORIA HOTEL

I WAS passing near the town when I remembered, and it was quite a few years ago, the days when I knew it well. Too well.

I have often thought of The Victoria Hotel, built, I imagine, in the years of that lady's realm. There was a conservatory where you could sit, often alone, in wicker armchairs, under a vaulted glass roof. There were blinds that could be pulled in the summer to keep out the sun. Chairs were scattered around the tables in groups of four. It was used mostly after dinner, or when it was warm and sunny. Families would sit there, or single people, as I was that first time. I was up for interview as a student at the town's university. I was staying on that occasion for just the three nights; it had been recommended as the best place to stay. I loved it. There was a sense of our colonial past. I was lucky; I was admitted, or I would not be telling this story. On the night that the Finals results were published, my friends and I went out on the town. We were drunk before dinner; we drank wine during the meal and kept going afterwards. I was staggering along the pavement, hoping to make it to the Victoria Hotel, when I could go no further. I made it to the police station and could go no further. I turned to the gutter and threw up uncontrollably. I became aware of large, black boots next to mine. It was a policeman. "Arrest me officer, please, please!" He was silent; he put his hand under my elbow, and led me inside the station. The sergeant was behind the counter, a little smile on his face. There were six others of my group, drinking from a large mug of tea. They smiled at me rather sheepishly. The sergeant poured from a large metal teapot and handed it to me. Tea had never tasted better. The Victoria had been shut for some time. They could not find a buyer; the only occupant now was the janitor; he was there to keep out bums, students and strays. He had to abandon the job when a student punched his nose. After that, he stayed in his room. At least, he had free board and lodging. Students had it all to themselves; those who knew about it. I banged on a window. Zoe looked through it and saw me. She opened the window and pulled me through. I was too drunk to help much. "Fancy seeing you". I got into bed beside her and crashed out.

I knew and liked Zoe. We had been friends in our last term. I had asked her, in the weeks leading up to the exam results, whether she would be my mistress when we got down to London. A friend of mine had a flat with a spare bed. She took my suggestion in a very matter sort of way. "Okay; as long as it suits you." I had finished one affair; she would be company to tide me over till I got established with my friend in London. I was quite frank about it. She just shrugged. That's okay." It didn't last long. She was an anthropologist and was off to an assistant lectureship at a Scottish university.

I remembered her for a year or two, and then only intermittently. I had a career as a scholar; French language and literature; and I was married.

Back here again, after so many years, I thought of Zoe. She would be middle-aged. Working probably. Anthropology wasn't it? She had probably forgotten me. Sad, really.

But we did meet again. We had come up to receive honorary

doctorates for outstanding achievements to scholarship. I said to Zoe, these second ranking places want to keep in the public eye; they have to do this sort of thing, don't they? We should feel honoured that they chose us, she said.

We laughed; that's worth a drink before we eat, she said. We got on well, after all these years. She had done original research in the field of anthropology, looking at the contrasting development between the tribes of Argentina in the middle ages. She had become the recognised source from which future scholars would have to start. I was doing the same. My big project, which would be the crowning achievement of my scholarly career, was a comparison of English and French fiction in the nineteenth century, decade by decade. It had long been recognised that from Balzac onwards, the French were a generation or more ahead of us in the portrayal of sex and body functions. Flaubert continued this, and Zola took it even further. It was not till after the First War that the English caught up. But no-one had ever made a detailed examination of author and decade. After a time I found it difficult; more demanding than I had expected. I consulted the work of the three established authorities, without giving the usual references as I should. No one would notice.

The next time we met was to be the last. We were both old and wrinkled. I needed two sticks to walk. She was just old and frail. Our alma mater was holding a small party for those of us who were left from the generation of sixty years before. This would be the last. Zoe was there, now Dame Connaught. "Zoe, I read it in The Times. You're a Dame. Congratulations!" "One tries to show a little modesty," she said. "I'm sure you deserved it." "Well, we had a good time back then," I said. Do you remember the night you pulled me in through the window of the Victoria Hotel? My God, I was drunk. Those were the days." It would have been indecent to remind her of how good she was in bed, back in London. "I'll tell you something," she said, though perhaps I shouldn't. That last time we met, there was a rumour going round that your doctor's dissertation was plagiarized; it was done quite cleverly, I heard, from three specific sources. Of course, I know you would never do such a thing." She looked at me with a steady gaze, waiting to see if I would deny it. I hesitated too long; she froze. "Well, I don't suppose it matters any more." She turned on her heel and walked away.

GERALDINE

ONE DAY, as a boy, he had seen a girl along the beach sitting with her family, as he was sitting with his. They were a short walk away. The girl looked about his age; she could be seven or eight. She was playing with a boy who looked two years older. The mother and father sat in deck chairs.

He, Simon Banks, did not rate girls very high on the interest scale. His sister, Sam, pestered him. Being two years older she thought herself superior and bossed him about. She had just refused to help him build a sandcastle. She lay with her back to him, reading a book. He walked along the beach.

"I'm Simon. Do you live here? My dad runs the post office."

The four of them looked at him.

"Come and sit down, Simon", the mother said. "This is Geraldine, and this is her brother Richard". She smiled at him and pointed to the two children. "We've come here for a holiday. We live in London". She looked nice.

She turned to the girl and said, "Geraldine, why don't you play with Simon?"

She had two ponytails and freckles on her face. He was too old to feel soft about girls. They were different from boys, but she would do to fill in the gap in his afternoon.

The next time Simon saw Geraldine, he was a strapping lad of thirteen. Again, it was on the beach. She stopped in front of him. "Hello, she said. I remember you. We played on the beach here when we were children. I forget your name".

"Simon. And you were the girl with freckles and ponytails".

She laughed. "I've still got the freckles, but I got rid of the ponytails".

Her hair was cut short all round her head, with a short fringe in front.

"Your dad ran the post office".

They went up to the top of the beach and sat on the sea wall and told each other their histories since that first time. Her father had brought his family and business to live here. It was where he wanted to spend his retirement. Simon's mum and dad now ran a family hotel on the front. He turned to point it out. His dad had sent him to a boarding school along the coast. He did not like it much but he got home at weekends.

Over the next few years, until he left school, he and Geraldine bumped into each other from time to time. They told each other about their schools. She sympathized with him for having to board; she was happy to live at home. Her brother was a bit of a pain, but he would soon be off on his own. Her parents didn't bother her too much, but she was looking forward to being fully independent as an adult.

The years passed. He liked the seaside town; it had all he wanted, why move? He was physically fit and liked the outdoor life. He was noticed: he was the young man they saw running on the beach. He had a body that attracted women, and the pleasure of them was there when he wanted it. Sometimes there were two or three he could turn to. He was earning good money from running a fitness centre; men only. Men were tougher and he could stretch them more. He came to know the right exercise regime for each client. He took them on the beach, weather permitting and often despite it. The beach gave him another job. The council paid him to sit on the lookout tower and help swimmers in trouble. He was happy in what he did.

The few times that he saw Geraldine, they stopped for a chat, they found now they had had little in common and not much to say to each other. She saw herself as a musician and Simon was just beefcake. She specially loved ballet music and she loved dancing. They were her world. Her father bought a hall for her and installed a small ballroom floor. There were changing rooms and showers. She taught ballroom dancing, and for young girls, the rudiments of ballet. She showed them how to dance to rock. It helped them to get boyfriends.

Simon and Geraldine had never had a serious friendship. As children, Simon had served her brief purpose, first as a playmate, and then to talk about schools. Neither of them now found a reason for knowing the other; when they passed in the street it was just, "Hi! How're things with you?" without waiting for an answer. He was body-centered; she had a life of the mind. It stayed like this for some years. They were now in their early thirties.

One day, Geraldine was knocked down by a car. It had run over her legs and done a lot of damage. One of the best local surgeons did what he could for this attractive young woman. Her accident had been in the local headlines. When she woke after the operation and saw what had happened, she yelled for the nurse.

Two came running. One sat on the bed and held her hand. The other said, "You've had a bad accident to your legs. The surgeon will be here this evening to tell you about it. You're not to worry, now; it could have been a lot worse". She gave Geraldine an injection. "This will help you relax".

She went to sleep and dreamt she was dancing as she had never danced before.

The surgeon made sure she understood everything he told her: the left leg would heal sufficiently to walk on but would be permanently stiff and awkward. The right leg was more serious. Her dancing career was finished, but there was so much that a young woman like her could do to build up a new life. She must think about that in a positive way. But first, he must see her again in four weeks, to review progress. He forestalled her question. "It would be wrong to conceal from you that amputation might be necessary – but only as a very last resort. Even that's not the end of the world, you know."

She spent much of the next four weeks weeping; then lying in silent despair. Her family did what they could but she refused to go back to live with them again. Independence was now more vital than ever. Her friends looked in but found they could not help her. "Well, if there's anything I can do for you, anything at all, you will let me know, won't you?" She wanted to be alone in her flat.

Simon had seen it in the local paper; it had even had its brief mention on the BBC news. It gave him a stab of pain, thinking how unbearable it would have been for him, cut off forever from the physical life that gave him everything he wanted. How could Geraldine ever get over it?

One day he went to see her. He rang her bell on the panel by the front door of her block. He rang twice, and waited.

"Who is it?"

"It's me. Simon".

"I'm in No 6, on the third floor."

A pause and then the door clicked open. He ran up the stairs and found her door open.

"Come in and shut the door. I'm in the front room".

She was in a wheelchair, her back to him, looking out to the beach and the blue sea beyond. He walked up to her and she turned her head to look at him.

"You see?" she said, and looked back through the window.

He pulled up a chair and sat beside her, in silence.

"You see", she repeated, "I'm in a wheelchair. I'm told I shouldn't. I must get used to hobbling about on crutches. Why should I? My life is finished. What difference does anything make?"

"You must feel it badly. I'd go nuts if I couldn't do the only thing I like doing. Getting out for a run. Working out. You know. Swimming and pulling people out of the water".

"Is that what you do? I knew it was something physical".

"Yeah, well".

They were silent, taking in what had been said.

He asked her, "What about your friends. You must have lots of good friends. Have they come and talked to you, offered to help? Cook, things like that?"

"They all came, at least once. They said to let them know when I wanted them. They'd be keen to do whatever I wanted. I only had to ask. I did not ask.

"That's all? What about your parents? Your dad has money, doesn't he? He must have helped".

"Oh, yes. Money's no problem. He had taken out a policy for me at the start. The premium's small at my age and he pays a small sum every month – just in case, he said. So now I'm independent, as far as money's concerned.

"And your brother? I forget his name".

"Richard. He's in America making piles of money. He rang twice the first week; now he rings every Sunday morning, 12.30 our time and 7.30 there. It's not too inconvenient and he can talk to mum and dad because they come to see me then, too".

"Tickety-boo".

"You don't have to stay, Simon; not if you don't want to."

There was a pause.

"I'll leave you in peace. I'll come again and see how you're getting on."

He let himself out.

He did come back and she was not sorry to see him. He told her to get out of the wheelchair. He would help her with the crutches. It was not long before she could cross the room unaided. He drove her to the hospital for her next physiotherapy. They told her she was doing fine; she must come back in four weeks and they would teach her to balance on her left crutch so she could shake hands. The nice young man would help her.

They had avoided anything too personal in what they said to each other. He told her about his work; the men who came to him for fitness training; what it felt like to strain every sinew of your body. He asked if she minded hearing about the things that were now lost to her. She said no. She remembered how it had been for her; the memory was less painful. She could think: dancers had to retire at some point, like athletes.

One day he asked her, "How's your love life? What do you do about sex? Have you got men to satisfy you?"

She was stunned. She looked at him. She was angry.

"I suppose you do it whenever you want. You get hold of a woman and it's just another workout when it's been too long since the last one".

"Yes", he said, "something like that. Why pretend it's so special?"

"You've never been in love?"

"No, and I'm not in a hurry".

"Well, we're very different people, you and me".

And they left it at that.

Geraldine had her music; she played the music she had once danced to and imagined doing it now. She played her music every day, and often it would be in her head, silently, as she sat by the window looking out to the beach and the blue sea beyond. She remembered every step and every movement of her body as she had once danced to the music. Sometimes, when Simon came in and found her like this, he would sit down beside her and listen as if for the first time, and wonder if he could like it. She asked him, did he like it? I might get used to it, he said. He liked its rhythm; there was rhythm in his exercises. He said he would bring her some of his music, see how she liked *Rock Baby Rock*. She did. She liked it so much she wanted more.

The thing about Simon was she still saw him as beefcake; but she saw now there was a lot more to him. No one else came so often; not her family, loyal as ever; and not her friends. No one else had helped her to walk as she now walked. She walked as well as she ever would. They walked on the beach and she got used to people watching her. He told her to walk faster and people watched her as she tried walking faster. They became known as Simon and the girl on crutches. They had always known Simon.

"It's funny", she said, "we met the first time as children, didn't we, on this beach. Look, it was just there, wasn't it?" she said pointing. It was. And he took her out in the rain so she would remember the feel of rain on her face. Some nights he came to sit beside her to watch television. They did not touch. I know you've got better things to do, she would say, all those women you can pick and choose from. He would give a small smile and a shrug. It's okay, he would tell her, they can wait. She was sad. Sad that he should feel about it that way. Sad, perhaps, perhaps frustrated that she was not that way too. Did she, she started to wonder, did she now want him?

They had been watching a film on TV. It was a love story; a sad one of unrequited love. They sat silent for a while after it finished. Simon let Geraldine wipe the tears away before turning to look at her. She turned to look at him and he could see her wanting him.

He whispered, "Would you like to?"

She murmured, "Yes".

He lifted her with great delicacy and carried her to the bedroom. He laid her carefully on the bed.

"Shall I undress you?"

"Yes".

Every slow, careful, oh so delicate movement that he made, his every shifting of her body as he stripped her, piece by piece, inflamed her desire and was erotic beyond her imagining. Finally, fully naked before him, she watched as he took off his own clothes, piece by piece, his eyes always on her eyes, and he folded each piece, one by one, slowly, placing them carefully on the chair. And then he eased himself onto her and she flung her arms round him. After, before he had eased himself off, she cooed in his ear like a mother to her child.

She was not a virgin when he came to her that first time. She had known three men in earlier days. She had thought she loved them, but love passed; and she was waiting for the right one. With Simon it had been perfect. She wanted him often and he was usually there for her. She knew it was not love, neither for her nor for him. She knew there were others and it was painful to know that, but she was ready when he was. It could not last. She thought she must tell him; but he told her first.

"Geraldine. I've been thinking. I've been living in a rut. We like each other a lot, don't we? But you know me, what I am. And you know you're not the only one. We don't go well together, do we? – we don't have a future, we're too different. And I don't want to spend the rest of my life bothering about love or marriage. I want freedom to do what I want, go where I want and just enjoy being myself. So I'm going."

And he went.

Simon saw the world, some of it. He picked up jobs where he could, doing his fitness thing on a beach in places where they spoke English. Canada first; Vancouver suited him. New Zealand and Australia were better and he earned good money. He could live rough, if he had to, but it never quite came to that. And there were always women. He was spoilt for choice; but he liked the blondes best, the tall and hungry ones.

And so it went on for some time. At odd moments he would think of Geraldine. He had been right to leave her; she was coming to take too much of his time and attention. He was too young to get tied down. He would build up a mountain of women to smother past memories. And that's what he did, until he was sure it had worked. Then he just kept going, as he had always done, working out and running and teaching men. It was his job in life; and in his leisure time, when there was nothing better to do, there were the blondes waiting.

It worked well enough, for a year or so. Then he rang her, on the spur of the moment.

"It's me, Simon. How're you doing?"

There was a pause before she replied.

"You want to know, Simon? Just out of the blue? I'm doing fine, just fine. I get out a lot; I'm walking faster than ever; I have friends and I like life. Why are you asking? Where are you calling from?"

He had meant to say, "I'm in Australia". It took him by surprise when he heard himself say, "Geraldine, I love you".

He waited, worried.

"No. Think what you're saying. Do you want to hurt me all over again? You left. It was your move and I was left with the consequences. Do you think I want to go through all that again?"

"Geraldine, this has just happened; I didn't plan it this way. Phoning you and then saying it. But I want to be home again. I want to be where you are. And you'll see that I'm serious. I won't ask or expect anything from you. I'll be there if you want me; even if you tell me you never want to see me again, I'll have to take it. But I'm coming. One day soon I'll ring your door bell and you can tell me".

No goodbye; he just switched off, stiff with shock. He had not intended any of that, not to ring her nor say any of what he had just said. He went into his bedroom and packed.

He rang her bell on the panel by the front door of her block. He rang twice, and waited.

"Who is it?"

"It's me. Simon".

"You know the way up".

A pause and then the outer door clicked open. He ran up the stairs; her door was open.

"Come in and shut the door. I'm in the front room".

He sat beside her. She waited for him to speak.

"I took myself by surprise, phoning you out of the blue like that and then saying what I did. But that on the side for the moment. Geraldine, what's it been like, I don't mean me not being here but what have you been doing? What have you been thinking about, how's life been treating you?"

"I'll come straight to the point. I'll never want you as I once did. I'll never trust you again with my feelings. When you left I decided to get along without you and that's what I've done and I've done it well. Does that answer your question?"

"It answers one of them and I'll not ask again. I've come back to stay. I shall pick up with my partner and get back to my business. You may see me around. We're likely to pass each other on the beach and we can talk if you want to. Now I'll let myself out."

He had not said sorry. At least he had spared her that.

He was right. They saw each other on the beach often. It was where they both liked to be. If they were near enough he would stop to ask after her legs, or comment on something. She had to acknowledge that he did not pester her. There was no hangdog, lovesick look about him. He did not gaze sadly into her eyes. No one would guess, looking at them talking, that he had asked her to marry him and been turned down.

"My partner did well in my absence. He had to work a bit harder, on his own. Some of my clients left, and he recruited new ones. But he was glad to see me back and now we're steaming ahead".

He laughed, "And we now take women; a dozen on the books so far. Bill Johnson, that's my partner, he takes the women, and he's qualified to take on the disabled. Do you feel like trying him".

Was she going to be a sourpuss?

"I'll give it a thought".

We left it at that.

So Geraldine went along for a session. Bill was good, and after a few weeks her physiotherapist noticed the improvement. He said she could come back in a year's time; he would not expect her to get any better, but would like to be sure she was not getting worse. She had a few more goes with Bill. She liked him and enjoyed the special workouts. If Simon saw her in the gym, he would walk across.

"How's she doing, Bill?"

"Great", he would say.

I must re-assess my relationship with Simon, she thought. Since coming back he has done everything right. I have never been bothered by a hint of him suffering, and I wonder if he is getting over it. Would he tell me if I asked? I have enjoyed his company, as before, and put to one side the storm of emotion that came after. Now, we were carrying on much as before, when we were just friends. This time, she felt, she could control things if they went bad. She could snap her fingers at him. That's what she thought.

So when he stopped her on the beach one day, she asked him, "What's the latest music these days? What do you listen to? I still have my ballet music; and I've branched out; I like jazz. I've even played *Rock Baby Rock*".

Naming that last one was a calculated risk. It was a marker in their past. How would he take it?

He stiffened, and slowly breathed out.

"Everything's all right, then".

He nodded and walked off. She had won that round.

It meant she could go further. She had him round for dinner. She cooked a chicken dish the way he liked. She paid more than usual for a bottle of wine. No, two bottles of wine. You could say she was teasing him. She wanted to see how far she could go.

She made sure they had plenty to talk about over dinner, the food, what they had done, local things, in the way old friends did. After the meal they sat side by side on the sofa. Off to the west the sun had ignited the clouds. She leaned back and waited.

"Well, Geraldine. It's so like the old days, I'm wondering, what's happening? I've been very patient; you must have understood that I've been waiting for the least sign of encouragement that we might get back to where I so stupidly walked out on you? I've cursed myself, you'll never know how much; I have regretted what I did".

He had turned to look at her.

"Geraldine, you're still the only woman I can love. Can we start again?"

He had come too far too fast. Thoughts flashed through her mind; Other couples came through similar bad patches and got over it. Wouldn't it be natural that Simon genuinely regretted what he had done? Hadn't she loved him, for a time? Would it be impossible ... was it too big a risk?

"Simon, I'm not prepared for this. I was thinking we've been getting along well as friends. I don't know if I could take it further. You have been very patient".

She put her hand on his arm, and left it there while she said, "I think we should avoid meeting for a while. See how we get on."

She stood up, and he stood. They looked at each other for a moment; Geraldine turned to the door and Simon followed. She opened the door and they shook hands and said goodnight.

What the hell, she thought later that night; live life, what could she lose? Her inner self, her soul, she would hang on to them. He had done it so why shouldn't she? Not as punishment, not just doing to him what he had done to her. She had liked it before and she missed it now. This time she would be ready.

She rang him one evening.

"Would you like to come round?"

It was not like the first time, more like carrying on from where they had left off, and knowing, this time, what to expect. It was good, still good. But I shan't stay in bed for the pillow talk afterwards. I'd say, best if you get back home now.

Neither of them talked of love. If he used the word, she would say, "not tonight, Simon. I'm happy this way, why be serious?

"As you say, my lovely one. We'll stay like this".

And so it went on.

173

One day Geraldine said, "Simon, I've been thinking. Now please, this is not because you once did it to me; but I'm still young and I've seen nothing of the world. Being disabled, it hadn't occurred to me, but look I get around pretty well, thanks to you getting me started. I'm confident, and I'll come back when I've got it out of my system. But I must be on my own. One day I'll ring as you did, just a simple message that I'm coming home. If you still want me, that's fine.; you should feel under no obligation. We can talk about it. I shall start with my brother, Richard, in New York. We've not seen much of each other over the years. It's time I got to know him, see how he lives; see New York. Then, who knows, I could go anywhere".

Simon was shocked, but what could he say?

"Intended or not, it feels like revenge".

"No!"

"You're going whatever I say, aren't you? I'll go now".

And she went.

She liked New York. She liked it very much. She soon found her way around town, mostly on her own. Richard worked hard; making money was the priority in his life. He was often late home from his work; or it might be a dinner, or assignation. He never said and she never asked. Over the two months that she spent there, the lady on crutches became a familiar sight in the galleries and concert halls. She went twice to the Metropolitan Opera. She would always remember their *Tosca*.

The cab drivers were darlings; they got out to help her and always had a joke. The only thing that did not work so well was getting to know her brother. He was always kind, solicitous, and gave her good advice. She imagined he would treat his clients the same. Before she left him, to see something of America, he worked hard to help her on her way. She thanked him, pecked his cheek, we must keep in touch, and she was gone.

It was expensive, of course, and she was careful to regulate her spending. Thank God for the insurance her dad had bought. She kept in touch with her family and they were glad to have news of Richard, in slightly more detail than usual. She had decided not to call or email Simon. She wanted to leave him a free hand.

She saw the west coast. She went on to New Zealand and Australia. Isn't that where Simon had gone? She made her way slowly, through the exotic countries of South-East Asia, then Sri Lanka, and finally by train through Europe, she got to Paris.

She rang Simon from Paris. Bill Johnson answered the phone.

"That's Bill, isn't it? Hi, Bill. Geraldine here. I'm calling from Paris. I shall be home tomorrow. Is Simon there?"

"Geraldine! How are you?" There was a pause. "Simon's away. He's gone abroad. Look, I have a letter for you. He asked me to give it to you if you got in touch. When shall I see you?"

She got back and read the letter.

"Geraldine, I've found there's a limit to how long I can wait. I have found someone else and it was love at first sight. Nothing complicated this time. We're just right for each other. We'll be in another country so you won't run the risk of bumping into us. I hope you work things out okay for yourself." That was the gist of it.

Geraldine settled down to a regular life. Bill was now running the gym on his own while looking for a partner. She went there once a week. For her domestic life, it seemed sensible to have a companion to live in. someone to take over the routine duties of laundry, cleaning and shopping. She still did the shopping and cooking when the mood took her. She was happy. She had started a novel about a man, an athlete who was paralysed after an accident – he bore no resemblance to Simon. She had given up on love. It was just too messy.

Her companion, Michel, was a nice young man in his middle twenties. He did without fuss whatever she asked him. There was a quiet finesse in his dealings with her. When the time came, he showed no surprise when she veered to a degree of intimacy – in a spirit of affection and mutual respect. Mistress and servant, in the nicest possible way. He had the tact to carry it off. She sometimes gave him a little present; and he knew how to reciprocate.

They lived like this for some time. They kept their mutual distance much as before; they were happy in what they did on their own, and in what they did together. What changed for them were their thoughts, back in their beds at night after being together. One day, Michel would return to his country and start a career. Geraldine knew she had been lucky; she might never find another Michel. Could there be another man for her, somewhere, some time? But she came back to it. Don't expect love. It had worked with Simon, up to a point. Love was the spoiler. Make do with paying for it when you wanted it.

She would wait.